Out of the Shadows

A Detective Amy Sadler Mystery: Book One

Michelle Arnold

ISBN: 1546778055

ISBN-13: 978-1546778059

www.amazon.com/MichelleArnold

facebook.com/MichelleArnoldbooks

For my dad, Charles Arnold, who passed down the writing genes

ACKNOWLEDGMENTS

Thank you to Kelly Daniel for making sure the medical stuff made sense, and to Claire Highton-Stevenson, Anna Rybak, Linda Pietrzak, and Shirley Fisher for serving as a sounding board

Prologue

She could hear him coming.

This didn't provoke the same emotions in her it once had. Once it had invoked terror. His arrival meant another injection, another cut. It meant he would do horrible things to her while she slept.

But she had come to fear more the hours she spent awake, immobile. Thinking. The cuff around her ankle bound her to the bed, and the bed itself was bolted to the floor. She could only move as far as the portable toilet beside the bed. She doubted she could walk anymore now even if she were set free. Her muscles had become atrophied from the time she'd spent (Weeks? Months? Years?) bound to this bed. Her body was skeletal now. Useless.

Sometimes, when she was asleep from the drugs he gave her, he must remove her from the room to bathe her. She would wake up damp, smelling of soap and shampoo. In some ways the thought of being limp in the tub while he washed her was even more disturbing than the other things she knew he did.

She had lost all control. Her body was not her own. She'd come to accept that the life she'd had before was gone. She just wanted her mind to go too, so she would stop remembering. She cried sometimes when she thought of how her family must feel, of her husband struggling to explain to their children why Mommy wasn't there anymore. For the longest time she had fretted over how her children were going to get home from school. She had been leaving to pick them up when he'd taken her, so they must have been stranded there. She realized, of course, that the school must have called Mark and that he would have gotten them. By now the school year had to have ended; perhaps the next one had begun, or the one after that. Perhaps by now they had all started their lives over without her. She didn't see how it could ever be any other way. Even if they found her, she was just a shell of the wife and mother they'd known. Mark couldn't possibly desire her anymore after the way she'd been treated, and she doubted she could take care of her children again. How could she, when she had no sense of self anymore? A mother had to have confidence, and she was simply an object. She had no voice.

She wondered sometimes if she was literally voiceless now or if it was all in her head. She hadn't used her voice in a long time, though she didn't know how long since she had no sense of time anymore. She had tried pleading with her captor in the beginning, explaining that her family needed her. Not only hadn't it moved him, but he'd given no indication that he even heard. He rarely spoke to her, and he never responded if she spoke to him. Eventually it had become so humiliating that she had stopped speaking entirely. Now she didn't even know if she was capable.

This was why she preferred the void to the time she spent alone with her own mind. It didn't matter what he did to her anymore, as long as she could sleep.

She closed her eyes when he came into the room and waited for the injection that would send her into oblivion. She couldn't stand to look at his face. She hated him, hated him with every fiber of her being, but she was powerless against him. It made her sick.

He pulled back the blanket that covered her and she shivered involuntarily. She had been naked ever since he brought her here. He always liked to stare at her before he got started, which was the worst part for her. She thought she could feel his eyes on her, moving down her body, and it made her skin crawl. *Just do what you're going to do,* she wanted to tell him, but she knew he wouldn't respond.

The injection never came. Instead she felt big, strong hands close around her throat, completely cutting off her air supply. She began to see stars floating in front of her eyes.

Finally, she thought. Finally.

Chapter 1

The phone rang insistently on Lira's bedside table, pulling her from a dream. She knew immediately from the ringtone that it was her boss, which at this hour could only mean one thing: there had been some sort of suspicious death somewhere in the county, and he needed her to go to the scene. She rolled over and reached for the phone.

"Dr. Ward," she said in her most professional voice, although she was a little hoarse from just waking up.

Arthur Myers, the Geneva County coroner, quickly informed her that there had been an apparent homicide in downtown Brookwood and that he needed her on the scene. She took down the information and promised to be there as soon as she could before hanging up.

She sat up in bed and rubbed her eyes. Homicide was never good news, but since it was here in Brookwood, that meant there was a good chance of Amy, her best friend who was also a homicide detective, being there.

That was when her dream came rushing back. It was about Amy. *Oh, no*, she thought. *This is going to be awkward*. It wouldn't be such a big deal if it had just been a sex dream. She'd had a few sex dreams about Amy in the past, and had never thought much of it. Amy was an attractive woman, and she was the person Lira spent the most time with, so a dream like that was no surprise. Lira wouldn't even have minded acting on one of those dreams in the interest of scientific inquiry if Amy were willing, and if she could be sure it wouldn't hurt their friendship. But she was pretty sure Amy would *not* be willing, and even bringing it up might hurt their friendship, so Lira had simply brushed the dreams aside. Last night's dream was going to be more difficult though. It was much,

much worse than a sex dream.

It was a *cuddling* dream.

Amy and Lira had cuddled up under a blanket in front of the TV in real life, but not quite like this. In the dream, Lira had been leaning against Amy with her head on her shoulder and her arms around her waist, and Amy had been slowly running her fingers through Lira's hair. Lira had felt unbelievably happy in the dream, and she knew Amy was happy too, because they were in love. That wonderful, crazy feeling of being in love flooded her again now, making her blush at the thought of seeing Amy at the crime scene. But that was silly. She couldn't fall in love with Amy. Amy was straight, wasn't she? The only person she'd dated in the three years Lira had known her had been a man, although she wasn't sure how serious that had been. Still, Amy probably would have mentioned it if she had any interest in women…then again, Lira didn't think *she* had. She had considered herself to be bisexual for years, although she had only dated men so far (when she dated, which wasn't often), and she didn't think she had ever mentioned it to Amy. She wasn't sure why not. She was positive Amy wouldn't have a problem with it, but somehow she'd just never seen fit to bring it up to her. Strange.

She got dressed and brushed her long, auburn hair in front of the mirror, her eyes drifting down to a framed picture on her dresser. The picture had been taken on Lira's 34th birthday, when Amy had gotten some people from work together to throw her a surprise party. No one had ever thrown Lira a surprise party before, but she'd always wanted one, and Amy must have remembered her mentioning it at some point. In the picture, Amy was behind Lira, her arms around Lira's waist, and they were both laughing. Amy looked gorgeous in her usual messy way. From her mother, who was African-American with some Cherokee mixed in, she had inherited a beautiful, light chocolate skin tone and raven-black hair; from her father, who was mostly Irish, she got wild curls and fiery hazel eyes. Her big, gorgeous smile was no one's but her own. She tended to charge around with a confident swagger that made her fit in well with the men she worked with, but she possessed a certain feminine beauty as well.

Lira always felt safe with Amy – not physically (although she supposed there was that, too. Who would mess with her when her best friend was a cop?) but *emotionally*. Lira was the product of a rather unconventional childhood, with a neurotic single mother who was also a well-known author. They had moved around a lot and her mother had always seemed suspicious of everyone, so Lira, who was shy anyway, never had many friends. She had become somewhat estranged from her mother as an adult in an effort to exert her independence and get some stability in her life, but she still struggled to relate to people. She just hadn't developed the right skills. But not long after she moved to Brookwood and started working at the county morgue, Amy had come barreling into her life while working on a case for the Sex Crimes Unit. She didn't seem to care that Lira was awkward and not well-liked. In fact, she seemed to take to Lira right away, and before long, they were spending a lot of time together outside of work. Then Amy had been badly hurt during an undercover operation gone wrong – it was the reason she'd moved to Homicide from Sex Crimes – and Lira had been the one to take care of her during her recovery, cementing their bond.

She'd never thought of Amy as anything other than a friend before, though. Had she? The phone rang again, interrupting her thoughts, this time with a ringtone that meant Amy herself was calling. Lira went back for the phone.

"Hello?" she said, trying to sound normal.

"Hey." Amy's voice was a little lower than usual, a bit raspy. She hadn't been awake long either. "Did you get called to the crime scene downtown?"

"Yes, I was just getting ready to go over there."

"You want me to pick you up?"

Always. "Sure."

"Okay, I'll be there in 15 minutes."

Lira hung up and looked at her Himalayan cat, Clea, who was still curled up on the bed. "I might be in trouble, Clea," she said softly. Clea just yawned.

***

Brookwood, a small Midwestern city of around 100,000 people, had been Lira's home for three years now, ever since she had completed her training as a forensic pathologist. Lira had been looking for a place to settle down, someplace where she could create for herself the stability she'd never had as a child, and Brookwood seemed perfect – not too big, not too small. It was right on a river and possessed a prestigious private college, Geneva University, that was well-known for scientific research. It was also home to the highly-ranked Geneva Hospital, which boasted a wide array of specialists and attracted patients from all over the country. The city had a diverse population and a vibrant arts community, such as you might find in a much larger city, but everything was much more compact and easier to navigate. Amy had lived here all her life and was quick to make Lira feel at home. Her own history made up for what Lira lacked.

Amy arrived just as Lira was finishing up her breakfast. Lira grabbed her bag, walked out of her prized 1914 brick bungalow, and climbed into the passenger seat of Amy's department-issued Ford Taurus.

"I wish the people who find dead bodies would sleep in a little later," Amy joked as she pulled away from the curb, sipping the coffee in her travel mug. Lira giggled, but she was still thinking of her dream. She kept stealing sidelong glances at Amy as they drove to the crime scene. Beautiful, lanky Amy was hunched over the steering wheel impatiently. She was wearing a leather jacket thrown over a t-shirt, and, as usual, her long hair was a glorious mess. Lira fought the urge to reach out and touch those unkempt curls.

What if I had that dream because I really am *in love with Amy?* she thought. *What should I do if I am? Would she be really mad if I told her?*

"You okay?" asked Amy. "You're awful quiet this morning."

"You mean I'm *awfully* quiet. But I'm fine."

Amy rolled her eyes. "Did you have a late night or something?"

"No, I got almost exactly eight hours of sleep." *Complete with cuddling dreams.*

Amy chuckled, putting the car in park. "Of course you did."

They walked to an alley that went behind several businesses, where a young officer was waiting for them at the crime scene, next to a barricade formed by yellow tape.

"Are you the responding officer?" Amy asked him.

"Yeah," he said, looking pale. "Mathew Bradley. I, um. I secured the crime scene, and I interviewed the witnesses…well, the people who found the body. They don't know who she is or what happened to her. There uh, there wasn't a pulse, but of course a doctor has to pronounce her."

"That's me!" said Lira brightly. "I'm Dr. Lira Ward, forensic pathologist with the Coroner's Office." She held up her identification.

"You're supposed to write that down," Amy informed him.

"Oh. Right." He fumbled for a pad of paper. "This is my first dead body."

"No shit," said Amy, flashing her badge. "I'm Detective Amy Sadler, Homicide. Where's the body?"

"Over there, behind that blue dumpster. Uh, Officer, uh…" He consulted his paper. "Detective Martinez is already here."

"Luis!" Amy yelled, noticing her partner behind the dumpster.

"Yo Sadler, what took you so long?" he hollered back, coming out into the light. Lira smiled and waved at the tall, muscular man in his thirties who had been Amy's partner since she moved to Homicide. Luis was the son of a fierce, independent woman who had brought her small children to the United States after escaping a controlling husband in Mexico. As a result, he had a lot of respect for strong women, and he and Amy worked perfectly together.

"I had to pick up Lira! What've you got?" Amy held up the crime scene tape for Lira to walk under before ducking under herself.

"Well, you might want to brace yourselves," he told them. "We haven't seen anything quite like this before."

"What, a body by a dumpster?" joked Amy.

"You'll see what I mean when you look at the body."

Lira carefully made her way to the back of the dumpster, pulling on gloves. At first glance, the body looked like so many others they had seen: a woman with reddish hair, perhaps in her thirties, with bruises around her neck. She was completely naked and had bite marks on her breasts, but unfortunately, that wasn't anything new. It didn't take long, however, for Lira to see what was so unusual about this case: there were tally marks carved into the woman's skin, all over her body. Some of the marks were white scar tissue, while others still looked red and angry. Several of the fresher ones showed signs of infection.

"What the hell?" mumbled Amy.

"I've been trying to figure out what the tally marks might mean," said Luis. "Some of them look old, so I'm thinking the killer must have had her for a while. Maybe there's a tally for each day of her captivity."

"Couldn't she just draw marks on the wall like a normal person?" complained Amy.

"I don't think she did this to herself," said Lira. "Some of the marks are in places that would be very difficult for her to reach, like her upper back. Even if she could reach with the knife or whatever sharp object it was, it would have been nearly impossible for her to make such precise tally marks without being able to see."

"That was my thinking," said Luis. "I think whoever did this was carving tally marks into her skin each day."

"She's in the early stages of rigor," said Lira, dutifully taking the liver temperature. "It's looks like she's been dead for about seven or eight hours."

"Well, if she's been missing for a while, there should be a report," said Amy. "We'll see if we can find her when we get back to the station."

Lira continued her examination while Amy and Luis went to talk to Bradley to find out more about when and how she had been discovered. Right now Lira's job was to pronounce death, take vitals to help her determine time of death, and take note of what condition the body was discovered in. She would learn a lot more when she did the formal autopsy later, and she knew Amy would fill her in on whatever she discovered over the course of her investigation. Still, as she looked at the woman's gaunt face and unseeing eyes, she found herself wondering about her. How long had she been held captive? What hell had she been through during that time? And who was she before? Who missed her?

Lira shook her head, not envying Amy her job of notifying the family. Her dream firmly out of her head for now, she got to work.

Chapter 2

Amy couldn't remember exactly when Lira had become the most important person in her life. Somewhere along the way, she'd gone from being just someone from work, to a friend, to her best friend; and somewhere in there, Amy had started developing feelings that went beyond friendship. For a long time, she had dismissed it as a meaningless crush. After all, everyone had a woman crush at some point, right? And if Lira Ward was part of your life, she was naturally going to be the object of that crush. Lira was the closest thing to a perfect human being Amy had ever seen. She could be a bit odd, but that only added to her charm. She was brilliant, beautiful, kind, and capable. There wasn't anyone else quite like her. Who *wouldn't* have a crush?

The problem was, it wasn't Amy's first woman crush. She'd never let the others develop into much out of fear of how her family would react. Amy's mother, Becky Sadler, had raised three children on her own after the death of Amy's father when Amy was twelve. Gus Sadler had been a firefighter, and he was hailed as a hero when a ceiling collapsed on him while he was trying to rescue a family trapped in their burning house. What the public didn't know was that Gus had never been much of a hero at home, often spending his nights off at the nearest bar instead of with his family. In the weeks preceding his death, Becky had learned he was cheating on her, and Amy and her older sister, Allison, had been convinced their parents were heading for divorce. When Gus died, Becky was taxed with trying to find a way to support her family when she had previously been a stay-at-home mom, as well as dealing with Amy's younger brother, Christopher, who began acting out in response to his father's sudden death.

Since then, Amy had tried hard to be the perfect daughter, to prove to her mom that she'd done just fine on her own. Amy didn't want to be like her father, a hero to complete strangers and a disappointment at home. She was a public servant as well, but she gave her all in both her personal and professional life. She was determined to make her family proud, and she was afraid being gay would ruin that. So she told herself it just wasn't an option, and she sometimes even dated men. Her last relationship had been with Tony, the son of one of her mother's friends. Her mom had thought he was perfect for her. Amy liked to fantasize that she was right, but if she were completely honest, Tony's best quality was that he lived two hours away. Most of their relationship was long distance, which made it easy to imagine that they'd be happy if they were really together. A year ago, he'd stopped contacting Amy, much to her relief. But not having anyone else to focus on made it even harder to ignore her feelings for Lira, which were too strong to really be just a crush. Amy loved her. She loved her more than she'd ever loved anyone.

But there was no way for their relationship to be anything other than what it was right now. For one thing, Lira was straight. For another, Amy's mom adored Lira now, but if she and Amy got together, she'd probably blame Lira for corrupting her perfect daughter. That would suck, because Lira was pretty fond of Becky. And, finally, Amy had a dream in her head for how the rest of her life should go. She knew it wasn't the most realistic dream, but it was one that would make everyone happy, so she had to do her part to try to make it come true. In her dream, she would finally find just the right guy, someone who loved her the way she was and didn't want to domesticate her, and they'd get married and maybe have a kid. Once she had the perfect guy to focus all her romantic feelings on, she would go back to just having regular friend feelings for Lira, and they'd be best friends for the rest of their lives. Lira would also find a husband who truly appreciated her, her kids would grow up with Amy's, Becky would babysit all of them, and everything would be perfect.

It was a nice dream, but lately Amy had been thinking it would make more sense to just marry Lira and forget about trying to find perfect guys for them both. They could have a kid together, if they wanted, and they could certainly make each other happy. People always said you should marry your best friend, right? Sure, Mom would freak out, but she'd get over it eventually, wouldn't she? She'd just be glad Amy was happy, and she'd probably be glad to see Lira happy too.

But there was the catch: Lira wasn't interested in Amy like that. She was just her loyal, devoted best friend, and Amy was not going to do anything to mess that up.

Still, nothing could stop her from grabbing every possible excuse to go next door to the morgue for the chance to see Lira. It was sort of ironic that the morgue had become a place of solace for her, but she and Lira had had many a good heart-to-heart over a dead body. And when she was working on a case as disturbing as this one, she really needed the breath of fresh air that was Lira, even if she *was* surrounded by the stink of rotting flesh.

"I got the full missing person report on the victim," Amy said as she strolled into the morgue carrying the flyer Luis had printed out. Two days had passed since the body had been found, and Lira had just texted Amy that she had finished the autopsy – mostly, anyway. Final results always took a few weeks. She didn't need to show Amy anything in particular, but Amy decided to come look anyway before they released the body.

"Good. I have cause of death," said Lira. She was outfitted in her usual autopsy gear: scrubs, gown, cap, safety glasses, mask, gloves, and shoe covers. Somehow, she still looked adorable.

"You go first."

"Based on the cutaneous bruising and her fractured larynx, it appears she died of asphyxiation due to manual strangulation."

"That's what I was expecting. And the rape kit?"

"Extensive bruising, tearing, and scarring of the vaginal wall indicate repeated sexual assault. I did find semen, which I'm having tested now."

"Great. With any luck, he'll already be in the system."

"We're also running a tox panel, because I found this." She pointed to the inside of the woman's elbow, where they were several needle marks. "I'm looking for something he could have used to subdue her. She doesn't have a lot of defensive wounds, and the only evidence I can find that she was physically restrained was the bruising around her right ankle." She lifted the sheet to show Amy what she meant. "It's consistent with the bruising you would see if someone was handcuffed for an extended period of time."

"Which is enough to keep her from running away, but not enough to keep her from trying to gouge the man's eyes out every time he raped her. He probably did drug her to keep her from fighting too much. Then again, the fight probably went out of her eventually." She held up the flyer. "Kelly Bruin, age 34. She had a husband and two kids, and went missing three months ago. When her husband made the report, he said their kids' school called him at work when she failed to pick them up. When he got home, he found her car in the driveway and her keys on the ground near the back door. Otherwise, not a trace. The theory was that someone grabbed her as she was leaving to get the kids from school. Most of the neighbors weren't home at the time, and those who were didn't see anything. Husband's alibi is iron-clad. No leads."

Lira took the flyer and studied it carefully. "She was missing for ninety-six days," she said.

"Yeah, so?"

"So that means Luis's theory on the tally marks is wrong. She has two hundred seventy-one tally marks on her body."

"You actually counted them all?"

"How could I make a complete report without counting the tally marks?"

Amy shrugged. "Well, you're right. Luis's theory is obviously wrong. We're back to the drawing board on that one. Do you think you can take impressions of the bite marks?"

"I can try, but bite mark analysis isn't very reliable. There's a lot of potential distortion with bite marks in human skin."

"I know; I just don't want to leave any stone unturned." Amy noticed Lira looking down sadly at the victim. "What's wrong?"

"It's just...I know there's no such thing as a non-violent rape, but this is one of the worst I've seen, with the extent of the damage to her vagina. I can't imagine the pain she went through. And to go through that every day for three months, while she had a family missing her...and the tally marks. He was likely trying to cut deep enough to make sure those would leave permanent scars, and he gave her an average of 2.8 marks each day she was with him."

"I know," said Amy, marveling inwardly at Lira's ability to do math so quickly in her head. "I just wish we knew what those marks *meant*."

Lira looked at her uncertainly, tilting her head slightly.

"You have an idea what they could mean, don't you?" asked Amy.

"I do, but I don't want to say it."

"Lira, if it could help the case in any way, you need to tell me so I can look into it."

Lira shook her head. "Even if I'm right, I don't think it would help the case. I think it would just depress me to say it out loud."

Amy sighed. "All right. Well, I'm going with Luis to notify the husband this afternoon, but first, why don't I take you out for lunch? We can both get a little break from this depressing case."

Lira smiled. "That sounds nice."

***

Amy braced herself before walking into the office building where Mark Bruin worked. This was the worst part of the job: notifying the next of kin. The only positive to this situation was that the man had to already be expecting news like this sooner or later, so it wouldn't be quite as bad as telling a man who had kissed his wife goodbye just hours ago that she was gone. Still, they were about to destroy whatever hope he had left.

Of course, one of the more cynical aspects of the job was that they weren't just delivering bad news. They were also here to carefully watch his reaction, to determine if this really *was* bad news for him. It seemed unlikely that he had anything to do with this – a man who hired someone to kill his wife usually wanted her killed right away, not tortured for a few months first – but anything was possible.

A secretary pointed Amy and Luis in the direction of Mark's office. Heads turned as they weaved their way around desks and cubicles. *Everyone here knows Mark's wife has been missing,* Amy thought. *They've all been waiting for this moment.*

The door to Mark's office was open. Amy walked in, Luis

right behind her, and saw him sitting at his desk, looking at his computer. A man had to earn a living, even if he was in the middle of the biggest personal crisis of his life.

"Mark Bruin?" said Amy cautiously.

He looked up, surprised. "Yes?"

Amy flashed her badge. "I'm Detective Sadler, and this is Detective Martinez with the Brookwood Police Department. Could we speak to you privately?"

"Yes, of course. I assume this is about my wife?" Mark said, politely but warily, as Luis shut the door behind them.

"Yes. Um, I'm afraid we have some bad news," Luis told him.

Mark instantly paled. "Did you find her?"

Amy nodded. "We found a body that we have confirmed to be hers."

"You're sure?"

"We confirmed it with dental records."

His face started to crumple. "I…when did she…die?"

"We found her the day before yesterday. She appeared to have been dead several hours at that point."

He started. "So she was alive all this time? We could still have saved her?"

"It's my understanding that the officers who were working the missing person case did not have any leads, but yes. She was alive until a few days ago."

Mark appeared to be searching for words he couldn't find. "How did she die?"

"She was strangled," Luis told him.

"Strangled? Who did this to her? Did you catch him?"

Luis shook his head. "We don't know yet, sir, but we're doing everything we can."

"That's what the other cops have been telling me the past three months. They all said they were doing everything they could to find her, but they didn't find her in time. What are you going to do that's different?"

"We have evidence now that we didn't have before," said

Amy gently. "The Homicide Department is now taking over the investigation. We're doing DNA tests and everything else we can to figure out who did this. It's not the same investigation it was when she was just gone without a trace."

Mark nodded uncertainly. "But she was gone three months. What was he doing with her all that time?"

Amy and Luis looked at each other, unsure how much detail they should go into.

"We can get you a copy of the autopsy report when it's complete, if you want," Amy offered. "But it might be best not to remember her that way."

"I..." Mark faltered. "Maybe I don't want to know all the details. I think...I think I can guess what he was doing. There's really only one reason someone takes a woman and holds her prisoner like that, isn't there?" He began weeping in earnest, his whole body shaking. There was no denying it: this was real grief. This man did not want his wife to be dead. He had nothing to do with it. That was when Amy noticed the family picture on his desk, the smiling face of the woman Amy had seen an hour ago on Lira's autopsy table. Next to her was a much happier version of the man in front of them, and with them were two small children: a little boy with a gap-toothed smile and a slightly younger girl. Both had red hair like their mother. Amy realized Mark had a job much more difficult than hers: he had to be the one to tell those two beautiful children that their mother was dead.

Amy looked around for a box of tissues and, finding one, quickly passed it to the grieving man. "I'm so sorry we couldn't have brought you better news," she said quietly.

"Where did you...find her?" he asked.

"In the alley behind Pickles restaurant," said Luis.

"She was the body behind the dumpster? Someone told me about that, but I said it couldn't be Kelly." He blew his nose loudly. "He just...threw her out like a piece of trash?"

"I'm sure you've been asked this before, Mr. Bruin, but this is important," said Amy. "Is there anyone who has shown an unusual interest in Kelly in the past? An acquaintance, an ex, even a stranger? Did she ever feel like someone was watching her? Did she have any kind of strange encounter with anyone?"

Mark shook his head. "She never said anything to me if she did. I told the police before that she'd had an ex who kind of stalked her for a while when I first started dating her, but that was years ago. I think they looked into it."

Amy nodded. "Do you have his name? It doesn't hurt to chase the same lead twice."

"Kirk Riley. I don't know where he lives, but the other cops should know."

"We'll ask them," said Amy. "Is there anyone we can call for you? Someone who could take you home and stay with you?"

"My mother," he said, handing his cell phone over.

Amy handed the phone to Luis, who went out to call Mark's mother.

"It would have been better if he'd killed her right away," Mark told her through his tears. "If he was going to kill her anyway, he should have done it right away instead of making her suffer for months first. She must have been so scared, so…"

"She may have been drugged," Amy blurted out, although she knew she shouldn't.

A tiny glimmer of hope appeared in Mark's eyes. "So she may not have known what was happening to her?"

"It's possible." That was a bit of a stretch. The woman was kept alive for three months; she couldn't have been doped up the entire time. But *damn*. The man was suffering so much. Amy felt horrible for him, and she just wanted to ease it as much as she could. She could only imagine how she would feel if anyone so much as laid a finger on Lira, and Lira wasn't even her wife, the mother of her children. Lira was just the friend she had inappropriate feelings for.

"I really hope she didn't," Mark said miserably.

Luis returned with the cell phone, and Amy stood up. "If you think of anything, even if you're not sure it's significant, do not hesitate to call us," she said, handing Mark her card. "I promise we will do everything we can to find out who did this."

***

"Well, I've been in Homicide less than a year, but I think this is my worst case yet," Amy told Luis on the way back to the station. "I hope we can keep the poor guy from finding out about the tally marks. He's already falling apart."

"We withheld that detail from the reporters, so unless it leaks, he won't find out that way," said Luis. "Was it any easier dealing with victims who were still alive?"

Amy shook her head. "They were suffering just as much as that poor guy. At least in Homicide, if we catch the guy, he goes away for life. In Sex Crimes we were lucky if they went away for five years."

"Yeah, that had to suck." Luis shook his head grimly. "I feel bad for him. I don't think I could take it if anything happened to Stella." Stella was his wife of just two months, a truly lovely person inside and out. Amy had been at the wedding, with Lira as her plus one.

"That's why I'm not married," she said. "I'm not brave enough to get that attached to anyone."

"Liar. You heart someone."

"I do not!"

"You do. I've seen the way you look at her."

"At *her*? I'm not gay."

He shrugged. "Call it whatever you want. I think she hearts you too."

"No she doesn't."

"So you admit it."

"I didn't admit anything!"

He laughed. "You just did! So ask her out already. She'll say yes. I've seen the way *she* looks at *you*."

"She doesn't. Does everyone think this?"

"Well, no one else is around you as much as I am." He pulled into the parking lot at the station. "I'd ask her out soon if I were you. She'll be thrilled. I'm gonna be at *your* wedding someday."

"You are so full of shit," Amy told him, blushing furiously.

She couldn't stop the image from entering her mind, though: how beautiful Lira would look in a wedding dress. How amazing it would be to call that woman her wife.

She shook her head to dislodge the thoughts. It would never happen, and anyway, she had a murder to solve.

***

Amy could feel the rope cutting into her wrists, her ankles. Her hands were tied together over her head. Her feet were tied separately, her legs spread apart. She could hear the man breathing, knew what he planned to do. She continued to struggle, but she couldn't get away, and she was losing hope that anyone would save her. Her own partner seemed to have abandoned her.

Her ribs ached from being beaten, and her head hurt from when he knocked her out. She hadn't been out for long; just long enough for him to strip her naked and tie her up. Long enough for him to find the wire, to realize she was a cop. That was why he had beaten her so savagely. He knew he was caught, knew she had backup somewhere, that he couldn't get away. If he was going to go down anyway, he might as well punish her first. But the backup wasn't coming, even though they must have heard *something* over the wire and should have come immediately when they lost communication. Now she wondered if she would even survive.

She took a deep breath and instantly regretted it. The pain was unbearable. Her ribs had to be broken. Who would hear her if she screamed? She heard him coming closer and decided to try.

The scream pulled her from sleep. She struggled against bonds that weren't there for a moment before realizing she was home, safe in her own bed. Without even thinking, she reached for her phone and dialed Lira.

"Amy? Are you okay?" said Lira's sleepy voice at the other end of the line.

"Yeah, sorry. I shouldn't have woken you up. I just…I had another dream about Flynn."

"I'm not surprised, with the case you're working on. And don't be sorry. I've told you before you can call me any time you need to. How are you feeling?"

"I'm okay, I'm just…" She could still feel the blind panic she had felt when she thought no one was coming to help her. She struggled to catch her breath, but couldn't. "I can't breathe."

"I'm coming over," said Lira.

"No, you don't have to—"

"I want to. I'll be right there."

The phone disconnected and Amy rubbed her eyes. She could still feel the rope cutting into her wrists and ankles, but this was tempered by the knowledge that she would see Lira soon. Her breathing evened out a little and she pushed herself out of bed, across the room to where Henry, her deaf golden retriever, was asleep in his dog bed. Henry wasn't much of a guard dog, but he did make a good companion. She knelt on the floor and ran her fingers through his fur, trying to focus on that instead of her dream. He opened his eyes and lifted his head slightly, looking confused as to why she was waking him up in the middle of the night. Seeing that she had nothing exciting to offer him, he put his head back down and lifted a front leg so she could rub his belly, which she did. The warmth of his fur brought her further into the present, further from that night a year ago when Daryl Flynn had attacked her.

There had been several attacks in the same part of town, all with the same MO: a masked man would enter a woman's home in the evening, sometimes when the sun was still up, and rape her at gunpoint. He chose women who lived alone and seemed to prefer young women with dark hair, so it seemed likely that he watched his victims for a time before attacking. Amy and the others in the Sex Crimes Unit agreed that the best way to catch him was to use an undercover cop as bait, and Amy was the best candidate. So she'd "moved" into an empty house in the neighborhood and simply gone about living a normal life there, coming and going on a regular schedule. She made sure to spend some time puttering around the garden each day so if the guy was watching, he would see that she was the type he went for. She felt very little fear about the impending "attack" because she knew he wouldn't get far. She was wearing a wire, and her partner, Mitch Wright, was parked down the street in a van listening in with another officer each night. The rapist reportedly went through some ritual each time he came into a woman's home in which he forced her to say she loved him and wanted to have his children before stripping her and tying her up. Once Mitch recorded enough of this ritual to use in court, he would come in and arrest the guy before he had a chance to touch Amy.

It took almost two weeks for Flynn to finally come after Amy, and maybe that was the problem. Mitch got bored just waiting for something to happen. Hugh Hardy had been on duty with Mitch that night, and they were missing some big game because of it. Hardy had brought a wireless radio, however, so they decided to listen to the game for a bit. As a result, they didn't hear when Flynn finally broke into Amy's "house." Amy still remembered the triumph she'd felt when he first came in, the relief that they were finally about to catch a serial rapist. She had cooperated with him up until the point when he told her to take her clothes off. Mitch and Hardy should have been there by then, but since they weren't, she decided to fight back. That was when Flynn hit her with the butt of his gun, knocking her out.

She had woken up naked, tied up, with Flynn ranting and raving at her about the wire, which he had destroyed. He then beat her viciously, breaking several of her ribs and puncturing a lung, before Mitch and Hardy finally had the sense to realize they'd lost contact with her. They rushed into the house just in time to stop Flynn from raping her. Amy never knew which was the worst part of the whole ordeal: the beating, the fear of being raped, or the betrayal by two people she should have been able to trust. Her only comfort afterwards had been the gentle presence of Lira, who had come every day to the hospital, and then to her apartment, to look after her and keep her company. Often she had stayed the night, climbing into bed beside Amy as if it were the most natural thing in the world. That way she would already be there if Amy had any bad dreams.

Mitch and Hardy had been disciplined for their actions that night, but they weren't fired, and Amy could not bear the thought of working with them again. She had worked with the department to get transferred to another unit, which was how she ended up in Homicide. She liked her new job. She'd always dreamed of solving murders, she loved working with Luis (who she didn't think would ever let her down like that), and she worked much more closely with Lira now. She just wished the transfer could have happened under better circumstances.

She heard a key turning in the door and knew Lira had arrived.

"Amy?" Lira called. Amy felt herself calm a little just at the sound of her voice.

"I'm here," she called back. Lira appeared in the bedroom doorway. Henry immediately jumped up and ran over to greet her. "Yeah, sure, you'll get up for her," Amy muttered.

"Hey buddy!" said Lira, bending down to scratch behind Henry's ears with a big smile on her face. Like Amy and everyone else, she still talked to the dog even though he couldn't hear anything. It just felt weird not talking to him. "Oh, what a sweetie," Lira crooned as Henry leaned affectionately against her, gazing up at her as if he were as enamored with her beauty as Amy was.

"Did you come here to see the dog or to see me?" Amy griped impatiently.

Lira looked up at her and smiled sweetly. "Mostly to see you, but I'm always happy to see my buddy!" She looked back down at the dog and rubbed his head.

"Okay, okay!" Amy squeezed past woman and dog into the kitchen. "Next time I come to your house, I'm going to talk to your cat instead of you and see how you like it."

"Clea will ignore you," Lira giggled, following Amy into the kitchen. "She's only affectionate with me."

"Hey, I was making progress with her the last time I was over."

"How are you feeling now?" Lira asked, pulling off her jacket to reveal her nightgown underneath. She must have jumped right out of bed and driven over when Amy called.

"My nerves are still on edge, but I feel better. Petting the dog helped. I feel bad that I dragged you out of bed and made you come all the way over here."

"You didn't make me do anything." Lira assessed Amy for a moment. "Sit down. Whenever I had a bad dream as a child, my mother would make me a nice, hot cup of tea."

"I don't have any tea," said Amy, sitting down at the kitchen table. Ignoring her, Lira filled a kettle with water, put it on the stove, got out two mugs, took a small cardboard box out of the cabinet, and extracted two tea bags. Amy's jaw dropped. "When did you sneak tea into my house?"

Lira giggled. "It bothered me that you didn't have any. This is caffeine-free, so it shouldn't stop you from going back to sleep. It should be soothing."

Henry sat next to Amy and put his head on her lap. "What did you have nightmares about when you were a kid?" Amy asked thoughtfully.

"When I was six I read a book about hemorrhagic fevers and had a recurring dream about blood coming out of my eyes and orifices." She turned the stove off as the water started to boil.

"Oh, yeah. Well, we all read that book in first grade, didn't we?"

"Very funny." Lira poured the water into the two mugs (Amy didn't have proper teacups, or a pot, although she wouldn't be surprised if Lira snuck those things in eventually) and brought them to the table. "I also had a lot of nightmares about playgrounds."

"Playgrounds?"

"Yeah." Lira poured some milk into each of their mugs, mixed in a little sugar, and sat down to drink hers. "I always felt anxious at recess because no one would play with me. I was always the new girl, and not only that, but I was the weird girl who kept her nose in a book and did science."

Amy shook her head sadly, carefully sipping her own milky tea. Lira was the only person she knew who made tea like this, but it was delicious. "Your mom shouldn't have moved you around so much. I thought writers were supposed to be hermits."

"She is now. She's only moved once since I left home. Now she's been in the same house for more than a decade. Why couldn't she have done that when I was a kid? I could really have used the stability."

"Well, stability isn't everything. I've lived in Brookwood all my life. People know me *too* well."

"It's better than starting over all the time, especially when you're a shy kid. My mom never saw it as a problem. She just wanted it to be her and me against the world. Sometimes I think that was why she moved so much, to keep me dependent on just her. But that would be a bit abusive."

"It would be very abusive. But maybe it wasn't that. Maybe she was trying to keep your father from finding you or something like that."

"It's possible. She won't tell me anything about him, so anything's possible where he's concerned." Henry moved from Amy to Lira, who scratched his head. "Do you want to talk about your dream?"

Amy shrugged. "It was the same old thing. I was tied up again. Naked. I just wish I could move past it."

"You have," Lira promised her, putting a soft hand on Amy's. "You had a horrible experience, but you've moved on with your life. You went back to work as a cop, and so far you've proven yourself to be just as amazing as a homicide detective as you were in the sex crimes division. I'm impressed by your resiliency!"

"So why am I still having nightmares?"

"It's only been a year. There are still some things your brain is processing about that night. It was a very traumatic event. I know you weren't raped, but what happened still qualifies as sexual assault, and that's one of the hardest traumas to cope with. It can take a while, but you're on the right track, and you're not letting it dominate your life. I'm proud of you."

"I'd probably still be afraid to show my face in public if I hadn't had you coming over here every day dragging me out of bed."

Lira smiled. "Nevertheless."

Amy swallowed the last of her tea and looked at the clock. "It's not quite two a.m. We both should try to get some more sleep."

"Sounds like a good idea." Lira put their mugs in the sink and started walking towards the bedroom.

"Wait, did you think I meant we should both sleep *here*?" Amy asked her.

Lira looked at her in surprise. "That's what I used to do after your attack. It's certainly faster than driving back to my house."

"Yeah, it is," Amy agreed. She padded into the bedroom with Henry at her heels. He curled up in his dog bed, and Lira casually climbed into the side of the bed she'd always slept on when she was looking after Amy after the attack. Amy had never stopped thinking of it as Lira's side of the bed. She slid under the covers on her own side, bid Lira good night, and let the sweet smell of her friend's herbal shampoo lull her to sleep.

Chapter 3

Lira frowned at her computer, deleted what she'd written, and tried again:

Mom-
I hope everything is well. I really miss you. I'd love it if you would come visit me sometime. I've lived in my house almost three years now and you still haven't seen it. I think you'd like it. I'm very happy there.

She stopped. It sounded too much like a guilt trip. Her mom did *not* respond well to anything she thought was a guilt trip. She deleted everything and tried one more time.

Dear Mom,
How are you doing? I really miss you! I was thinking maybe you could come to visit around the end of the month? I have some vacation time and I would love to show you around Brookwood. I know it's not a big city, but there's actually a lot here with the university and everything. There's a big history museum you would love. I also think you'll like what I've done with my house. Maybe you can get to know Amy a little better too.

Lira paused. Was it appropriate to mention Amy? She didn't want to give the impression that Amy was anything other than a friend, but she *was* extremely important to Lira. Her mother had only visited Brookwood once since Lira had moved here, and that had been a stop on a book tour, so she had only been in town one night. She hadn't even had time to see Lira's house, but she'd had dinner at a restaurant with Lira and Amy. She didn't seem to like Amy, but that was no surprise. She'd never liked any of Lira's friends. This was different, though. Lira *needed* her mother and Amy to get along. They were her two favorite people. She decided to leave Amy in the email.

I hope you can come. If the end of the month doesn't work for you, let me know when would be a better time. I'm really looking forward to spending time with you!
  love, Lira

She read over it one last time, accepted that it would never be perfect, and hit send. She immediately felt like she would throw up. She'd been trying to convince her mother to visit ever since she moved to Brookwood three years ago, but had no luck other than the book tour stop. She was perplexed as to why the mother she'd once been so close to just couldn't be bothered with her anymore.

There was a tentative knock at her office door. She looked up to see her new resident, Clarissa Hill.

"I have DNA test and tox screen results from Kelly Bruin's autopsy," Clarissa said. She'd only been here a few weeks, but Lira liked her very much so far. She was a quiet, introspective young woman with rich ebony skin, glasses, and long dreadlocks that she always kept tied back. So far she had proven herself to be thorough, observant, and sharp-witted. She was exactly what they needed in the morgue, and Lira was already starting to hope she would consider a career here once her residency was finished.

"Thank you, Clarissa," said Lira, reading over the report. She glanced at her watch. "I'm just going to run this next door to Detective Sadler."

Lira didn't really have to go all the way to the police station to give Amy her test results, but she often did anyway. Anyone else she would email, but somehow no one seemed to question her commitment to giving Amy results in person. When she arrived this time, she found Amy and Luis hunched over a computer screen. Neither of them looked happy.

"What's going on?" Lira asked.

"Another woman's gone missing," explained Luis. "We think it's the tally marks guy again."

"She *is* his type," agreed Amy, motioning to the picture on the screen of a redhaired woman in her mid-thirties. "Her name's Jennifer O'Malley. This one lives alone, but her parents reported her missing. They found her keys and purse next to her car, in her building's parking lot. No witnesses. No way to be sure if it's the same guy, but the circumstances of her disappearance are so similar to Kelly Bruin's."

"We could really use the DNA results," said Luis.

"Well, I have them, but it isn't going to help much," said Lira. "There was no match in CODIS. Whoever he is, he's not in the system yet."

"Shit," mumbled Luis. "Did you get the tox screen too?"

"Yes. He was injecting her with ketamine."

"Well, that explains why she didn't fight much," said Amy. "That's a common date rape drug. I saw it when I worked in Sex Crimes."

"Exactly," agreed Lira. "She may not have even known where she was while under the effects of the drug. On high enough doses, people enter a dissociative fugue state where they lose all sense of time and even self. Hallucinations and paralysis are common. On even higher doses, the user, or victim in this case, is completely sedated. The only good news is that she may have had no concept of how long she'd been there, and she likely had little memory of the things he did to her."

"Great," said Amy. "So at least our new vic can look forward to seeing rainbows and unicorns while she's actually being raped and carved up."

"Well, a person's state of mind can affect whether they have a 'good trip' or 'bad trip,'" Lira pointed out. "I doubt she's in a good state of mind, so if she's having hallucinations, they're probably terrifying."

Amy sighed in frustration. "Then we damn well need a lead so we can get her out of there in a hurry."

Lira smiled grimly. "I wish I could have been of more help."

"It's not your fault the killer's DNA isn't in CODIS," said Amy. "Listen, we gotta go interview this new lady's family, but when I get back, I was thinking maybe we could grab some Chinese food and go back to my place?"

Lira smiled again, for real this time. "I would like that. Let me know when you're back."

Before she got on the elevator, Lira looked back and watched for a minute as Amy discussed the case with Luis and a few other cops. She knew they didn't have much to go on yet, but she had complete faith in Amy. Amy would not rest until they got to the bottom of this. *She's never been with anyone who appreciates her as much as I do,* Lira thought impulsively. Tony certainly hadn't. He dropped her completely after her attack last year, apparently not knowing how to handle the situation, when he should have loved her more than ever for being so brave. *She deserves to be appreciated. I could give her that.*

As she walked back to the morgue, she decided she was going to talk to her mother about Amy. That was the normal thing to do, right? She was in love with her best friend, and she didn't know what to do about it, so she should ask her mother what to do. She didn't think her mom was really the love expert since she'd never married and had, as far as Lira knew, not even dated since getting pregnant with her, but that didn't mean she couldn't have any good advice. Maybe it would bring them closer again if Lira was more open about her personal life.

Her heart lifted when she saw her mother had already responded to her email. She opened the reply and read:

Lira,

I'd love to spend time with you, but I'm so busy working on my next book. I don't think I can get away anytime soon. I've seen the pictures of your house and it really is lovely. I'm not sure it would be much different in person though. I know you say you want me to be part of your life now, but I'm not sure if you really do. You've pushed hard to have your independence. You have a career I don't understand. This friend you're always going on about knows you better than I do at this point, so spending time with her would just be awkward. And I fear the day is coming when you'll decide you want nothing to do with me at all anymore. If you truly want to see me, you'll use your vacation time to come out to Connecticut. I am always here for you.

love, Mom

Lira's heart sank again. She closed the email and began to cry quietly.

Chapter 4

"So Jennifer O'Malley's parents aren't aware of anyone who might have been stalking her or might have wanted to hurt her," Amy told Lira as she drove away from their favorite Chinese restaurant. "They're also unaware of any potential connection between Jennifer and Kelly Bruin. They ran in completely different circles. Every lead we've tried to chase down for Kelly has come up empty, so it's looking more and more like she was killed by someone she didn't know. And if Jennifer was taken by the same guy, she probably doesn't know him either. If he's not someone either of them knew, and they didn't know each other, then we literally have nothing to go on to find the creep. And if he's abducting women he doesn't know just because they fit the physical type he finds attractive, he may be on his way to becoming a serial killer. In other words, this case is all kinds of bad. It really doesn't get any worse than this."

She stopped at a red light and looked over at Lira, who was being uncharacteristically quiet. She saw that Lira had opened the glove compartment and was taking things out.

"What're you doing?" Amy asked her.

"I'm organizing your glove compartment."

Not a good sign. Compulsive organizing meant Lira was upset about something.

"Yes, I see that. Can I ask why?"

"It's a mess." Lira examined a little-used tube of lipstick. "Amy, I'm just going to throw this out. It expired three years ago. Where's your trash bag?"

"I don't have one."

"Then what do you do with your car trash?"

"As you can see, I stuff it in my glove compartment."

"I'm going to get you a car trash bag. This is very unhealthy."

"You do that, Lira," Amy said in resignation as she parked her car in front of her building. "I'm going to walk Henry before I eat, but you can start without me if you want."

By the time Amy got back in with the dog, Lira had set out their food on the kitchen table, complete with real dishes, which was more than Amy had planned on doing. She gave Henry his dinner, sat down to eat, and noticed Lira sorting the vegetables on her plate by color.

"Are you going to tell me what's bothering you?" she finally asked.

Lira sighed. "Well, I've been e-mailing my mom, trying to get her to come visit me, but she won't."

"Why not?

Lira shrugged. "She says she's busy writing her next novel and I should visit her instead. But she always says something like that. She also keeps saying that I wanted my independence, so I shouldn't be upset that she's not coming to visit, and that someday I won't want anything to do with her at all anymore."

"That's strange. Why would she think that?"

"I don't know." Lira picked at her food. "We used to be so close. She was proud of me when I chose to study pre-med in college, but she's been different ever since I told her I wanted to be a pathologist. She tried to talk me out of it. She said it was disgusting to work with dead bodies, and that I wouldn't really want to work that closely with law enforcement. But it was what I had my heart set on, and when she realized I wasn't going to change my mind, she acted like I had betrayed her. I know a lot of people don't understand why anyone would work in my field, but I don't see how she could feel strongly enough to distance herself from me over it."

"Maybe she doesn't like you working in pathology because she's afraid you'll search the system for DNA that's similar to yours."

Lira nodded, looking down. "I've thought of that. I won't say I haven't been tempted, to see if I can find out who my father is."

"So why haven't you?"

"It would be an abuse of my position to use it for personal research."

"Nice try. What's the real reason?"

Lira looked up. "I'm afraid I'll actually find something."

"I suspected as much. You wouldn't come up with anything unless he's actually in CODIS, and that's not really good news."

Lira shook her head. "I certainly hope he's not. But it's a thought I've had a lot over the years. Every time I asked about him, all she would say was that I was better without him in my life. What if their relationship was never consensual and she just doesn't want to tell me?"

"You're worried you're the result of rape?"

"How do I know I'm not?"

"I guess you don't know, but I don't see why she wouldn't tell you. It isn't like it would be your fault. Whoever your father is, you're not responsible for any of his actions."

"I know that, but...maybe I remind her of him. I probably look like him. I've never looked that much like her. Maybe she doesn't want to be around me because of the memories it brings up."

"Lira, don't be ridiculous. You couldn't possibly remind someone of a rapist. And even if that *is* how you came to be, she chose to keep you. Obviously you're worth it to her."

"I think I used to be. I'm not sure anymore."

"Of course you still are. She's just busy, and she's trying to let you live your own life."

"But why does she think I won't want her around anymore? I wouldn't judge her if I found out she was raped."

"Maybe that's not it. Maybe she was involved with someone she shouldn't have been. Or maybe your father is a really nice guy and she's afraid you'll be mad when you find out she kept you from knowing him."

"Well, if he's a nice guy, it's probably safe to say he's not in the system."

"Probably not. Maybe he's a pathologist, or a cop, or a coroner! Maybe Arthur's your dad!"

Lira laughed a little. "I don't think he's old enough to be my dad. And I don't look anything like him."

"Well, whoever your dad is, whether he's a good person or not, he passed on his best genes to you. You're really an incredible person."

"Thanks," said Lira softly. "Really, I don't mind not knowing who he is, as long as I can be close to my mom again. I've always wondered about him, of course, but she was enough for me. She was always enough. I don't want to lose her over this."

Amy watched Lira gather their dishes and take them to the sink. Her heart ached for her. She couldn't imagine why anyone wouldn't want to spend time with Lira. She also couldn't imagine what it was like to have a mom you rarely saw. Her own mother bugged her about this or that every single day. Hell, she bugged Lira about stuff now, ever since she decided Lira was being under-mothered. Lira seemed to like it, though, and as much as Amy's mom drove her nuts sometimes, she loved her for that.

"Well, I only met your mom once, and I didn't get the impression she liked me much," said Amy, following Lira to the living room couch. "But I did get the impression that she cared about you. I don't know if that helps or not, but I'm certain she loves you."

"I know she does, in her own way. I *am* her only child, after all. But...sometimes I just feel like no one actually loves me for being *me*."

"Lira! How can you say that? Everyone loves you! *I* love you!" Amy put her hand on Lira's face. "I love everything about you. I love you more than *anything*." Impulsively, she leaned forward and kissed Lira, ever so gently, on the lips. She pulled back then, certain that she had made a mistake, but Lira didn't look upset. She was just staring at her with those big, green eyes, and she looked so...*trusting*. So Amy kissed her again, and again and again, until the next thing she knew Lira was lying back on the couch and she was on top of her, covering her face with kisses. Suddenly overwhelmed, she wrapped her arms tightly around Lira and just buried her face against her neck for a moment.

"Amy," Lira murmured, "I love you too."

Amy lifted her head and looked down at Lira. "So you want this?"

Lira smiled, her family predicament momentarily forgotten. "Yes. I do."

So Amy resumed kissing Lira, as Lira twined her fingers in Amy's hair. It didn't feel like it could be real. She'd wanted this for so long, but she'd never believed for a minute that it could ever be possible to *have* it. She was afraid to stop, to even come up for air, for fear that it would be over as quickly as it had started. But then Amy felt Lira's hand moving towards her breast and pulled back in surprise.

"I'm sorry," said Lira. "I didn't mean to—"

"No, no, you're fine. I just wasn't expecting anything like that."

"I just...I've thought about this, a lot. I've wanted to do something like this with you for a long time. I just didn't think you'd ever want to."

"You've wanted to do...sexy stuff? With me?"

Lira nodded. "You *are* sexy." Her hand slowly moved back to Amy's breast, and Amy didn't pull away this time.

"Well, you're pretty hot yourself, but I never thought you were, you know, into women."

Lira smiled, her other hand moving down to grip Amy's firm ass. "I've always been attracted to both men and women. I've just had more opportunities with men."

Amy hesitantly fingered the soft material of Lira's blouse, inching towards a voluptuous breast. Lira didn't seem to mind, so she inched a little more until her hand was stretched out over Lira's breast, covering as much ground as she could, which was only about half of what was there. It felt amazing. "So ...you're bi?"

"Yes." Lira stroked Amy's nipple with her thumb, and Amy

uncertainly did the same to her.

"Why didn't you ever tell me that?"

"I'm not sure. I think I was afraid that if you knew, you'd figure out I was attracted to you, and I didn't know how you'd react." She lifted her head and kissed Amy's jawline, her lips soft and gentle. Amy couldn't remember ever being this turned on before.

"Well, I...I wouldn't have had a problem with it," Amy replied weakly. She kissed Lira's face again. She couldn't resist, now that she knew she was allowed.

"I thought *you* only liked men," said Lira.

"I like *you*." Amy recaptured Lira's lips, and this time Lira's tongue requested entrance, which Amy granted. She felt herself sort of melting into Lira, the two of them becoming one person, and it was hot. It was *so* hot. Amy had never felt quite like this before.

But eventually, they had to pause for air. Amy looked down at Lira, who was smiling up at her adoringly. "Perhaps we should move to the bedroom?" Lira requested sweetly.

"You're sure?" Amy asked her.

"I'm sure."

Amy got up and helped Lira to her feet. They walked together to the bedroom, where Lira pulled Amy down onto the bed with her. Amy hesitated.

"Lira, I want to do this. I do. But...maybe I should read a manual first or something."

Lira laughed. "A manual? Since when do you read the manual for anything?"

"Well, this is...major."

"You don't need a manual. I'm a woman. I have the same genitalia you have. You know what to do."

"But I've never—"

"Amy." Lira kissed her. "You really love everything about me?"

"Yes."

"Then show me."

Amy had never been good at saying no to Lira, and Lira in

bed was a different story altogether. Heart pounding, she slowly unbuttoned Lira's blouse, then unhooked her bra and slid it off, revealing two full and absolutely perfect breasts. It actually wasn't the first time Amy had seen them, but before she hadn't been permitted to stare, or to touch. She tentatively cupped them in her hands, feeling the nipples harden under her thumbs. She leaned down to kiss Lira's right breast and then slowly slid her tongue around it. Lira moaned softly. Amy traveled around with her tongue, eventually bringing it up to Lira's nipple and swirling it around. Lira moaned a little louder. Amy began to suck on Lira's nipple, which caused Lira to seize Amy's head and hold it firmly in place. So far, so good.

Amy moved to the left breast, her fingers lightly moving up and down Lira's sides, feeling her shape, the softness of her skin. She was taken with the urge to kiss Lira everywhere, to make her feel how loved she was.

But then Lira announced, in her most commanding voice, "Amy, I want you to go down on me."

Amy was immediately filled with terror, but it was too late to back out now. She carefully removed Lira's skirt and panties. Now Lira was completely naked, while Amy was still wearing her suit from work. She knelt down between Lira's legs and tenderly, uncertainly, kissed her. Lira's hands immediately seized Amy's head again, urging her on. *What the hell have I gotten myself into?* Amy thought. She moved her tongue slowly around Lira's pussy, tasting her wetness. *Damn.* She liked the way she tasted, liked being this close to her. She wanted more than anything to make Lira feel good, but she didn't know if she could do it. She had to try, though, so she touched Lira's clit with the tip of her tongue and, hearing Lira gasp, began licking very softly, and then harder.

"Amy, use your fingers too!" Lira cried.

Amy was on the verge of having a panic attack, but she obediently wet her fingers and slid two inside of Lira. It was a bit like entering some sort of sacred place she wasn't sure she had the right to, but there wasn't time to ponder that now. She had to focus on what she was doing. *If she doesn't come soon, I'm going to pass out from the effort*, she thought. *And I am definitely reading some kind of manual before I do this again.*

Fortunately, within minutes Lira's back was arching from her orgasm, her hands clutching Amy's hair. Amy crawled up to her pillow and collapsed. Lira turned to face her, a smile lighting up her face. "Now I get to do you!"

Amy rubbed her face, then realized she was smearing Lira's wetness on herself. "Lira, you don't have to."

"But I want to! Don't you want me to?"

Amy thought for a second. "Yes. I want you to. But—"

"Then I'm going to. I think you will find I'm quite dexterous." Lira immediately busied herself with removing Amy's clothing.

"Have *you* done this before?" Amy asked, still amazed by Lira's nonchalance.

"No, but I've read a few books about lesbian sex, so I understand the basic principles."

"So *you* read a manual."

"If you want to call it that." Lira finished discarding Amy's clothes, climbed on top of her, and pressed her lips to Amy's neck, planting a trail of kisses until she moved down to Amy's breast.

"So why did you read all these lesbian sex books?" Amy asked, suddenly gasping as Lira took her nipple into her mouth. She wrapped her arms lightly around Lira. "Oh, that...that feels good."

Lira sucked for a minute and then let go. "I read them because I was curious, and because I thought I might get a chance to do it someday. Hasn't anyone ever sucked your nipple before?"

"Well, yes, but not...somehow, not as well as you did."

Lira smiled and began moving downwards. Amy tensed. "If I'd known we were going to do this, I would have shaved my legs more thoroughly."

"It's okay. I don't mind." She was getting closer to her destination, and Amy became more nervous. This was where it always fell apart. She'd get psyched up, thinking something good was going to happen, and always end up disappointed.

"No one's ever given me an orgasm before," she blurted out.

Lira looked up in surprise. "Never?"

Amy shook her head. "Well, *I* have. But no one else ever has."

"That's a shame," said Lira, looking truly sympathetic. "But I accept the challenge."

Her soft fingers slid down between Amy's legs and began to lovingly caress her pussy. Amy had never been touched in quite this way – not in such a tender, sweet manner – and she was surprised by how emotional it made her.

"You're pretty wet, so that's a start," Lira murmured. "Do you like this?"

"Yes," Amy admitted. Without even thinking about it, she spread her legs a little further apart to give Lira better access. *This can't be real. Can it?*

Lira lightly stroked Amy's clit, watching her face carefully for a reaction, then dove down and replaced her finger with her tongue.

"Oh *fuck*," Amy shouted, a bit louder than she'd meant to. "Lira, that's…that's good."

She could feel Lira smile against her. Amy looked down in amazement at the beautiful woman who was between her legs, happily tapping different rhythms with her tongue. It felt so sweet, so incredible, so…terrifying. What if she still couldn't come? Would Lira still want her?

"If you can't make me come, it's not your fault," she told her.

Lira stopped what she was doing and looked up patiently. "I'll get you there," she promised. "But it'll be a lot easier if you relax. Stop worrying and let me take care of you."

Amy nodded. "I'll shut up."

"I'm happy to address your concerns, but my mouth needs to be busy with other things right now. Would you like me to do what you did to me? Give you both vaginal and clitoral stimulation?"

She did. She really did. She wasn't even going to complain about the fact that Lira sounded like a medical textbook. "Sure, you can try it."

"Okay. Just relax. You're with someone who loves you. Whatever happens, that's not going to change."

Lira carefully wet her fingers and went back down. Amy looked at the ceiling, trying to relax as Lira sucked her clit back into her mouth and carefully slipped a finger into her. She curled the finger forwards and Amy involuntarily let out another yell. "Oh *fuuuuck*, Lira! That's good! That's good!"

Lira slipped in another finger and began moving in and out, still swirling Amy's clit with her tongue. Amy had never felt anything like this before. She needed to hold onto something, but she didn't know what, so she seized the bedsheets and braced herself. As Lira thrust deeper and deeper, Amy found herself thrusting back with her hips, wanting to take her in more. She kept waiting for that moment of disappointment, the moment when she would realize that what she had hoped to enjoy wasn't fun after all, but that moment never arrived. Instead, something very, very different happened.

Amy was suddenly filled with the strongest, sweetest orgasm she could possibly have imagined, far better than anything she'd ever done to herself. It seemed to spread through her entire body, filling her with such pure ecstasy that she was certain she had actually touched Heaven. Living people weren't meant to feel this kind of elation, were they?

When it was over, she felt like her body was sparkling. She felt peaceful. *I've been doing this wrong*, she realized. *I've been doing it all wrong.*

Lira crawled up to her usual pillow and stretched out, admiring Amy with a pleased smile. "Did you enjoy that?"

"Honey, the *neighbors* probably know the answer to that question."

Lira giggled. "I gave you an orgasm."

"You sure did. Congratulations. You are the first." She pulled Lira into her arms and stroked her hair. "I hope I satisfied you just as much."

"Oh, you did. I know you were scared, but you did beautifully. I needed that."

Amy turned the lamp off and hugged Lira closer. "Do you feel loved now?" she whispered.

"I do," Lira whispered back, and then she fell asleep with a smile on her face.

Amy lay awake for hours, her heart still racing. She felt simultaneously ecstatic and terrified. She finally had what she'd wanted for a long time: she had professed her love for Lira, and it didn't scare Lira away. Instead of being scared, she was *happy*. It was the best possible outcome. If this meant they were a couple now, it would make Amy's life a whole lot easier. Now when she felt like kissing Lira, she could just do it. If a guy hit on Lira, she could actually say, "Back off, she's mine." But she couldn't stop wondering if Lira really loved her the same way, or if she was just accepting the comfort that was offered to her in a vulnerable moment. Had Amy taken advantage of her? Would Lira still feel the same way tomorrow, or next week?

Amy ran her fingers through Lira's soft, silky auburn hair. She looked so beautiful, so peaceful. Amy finally gave in to the moment and just let herself relax. She kissed the top of Lira's head, inhaling the scent of her shampoo. "I love you," she whispered, hoping the words would make their way into Lira's dreams.

Chapter 5

The following morning, Lira had the rare experience of feeling like she was waking from a lovely dream, only to discover that it hadn't been a dream after all. Her beautiful Amy was sound asleep, completely naked, with one arm thrown over her head and the other around Lira, whose head was resting on Amy's shoulder. Her memories of the previous night came rushing back. Amy *loved* her. She loved her, and their relationship had moved into something beyond friendship. The sun was just coming up, but she knew they would need an early start today, so she decided to go ahead and wake Amy.

Amy's eyes registered surprise when she first opened them, but then she smiled—or at least, she did what passed as a smile for her this early in the morning. "Hey," she said.

"Good morning!" chirped Lira, leaning forward to kiss her. "I know it's early, but I need time to go home and get clean clothes and feed Clea before we go to work."

"Yeah, that's smart," said Amy, looking at the clock. "I'll make coffee." She sat up, touched Lira's hair, and reached for her cell phone. "Oh, crap."

"What is it?" asked Lira, struggling to find all the pieces of the outfit she'd had on the day before.

"It's my mom. She drove past your house and saw your mail from yesterday sticking out of the box, so now she's worried. She has *got* to be the nosiest person alive." Amy got up and wriggled into her robe while typing one-handedly.

"What are you telling her?" Lira realized she was putting on Amy's underwear, but decided it didn't matter.

"I'm telling her you crashed at my place and everything's fine."

"That's all?" Lira was slow about buttoning up her shirt. She could see Amy staring at her breasts, and she liked it.

"What do you want me to tell her, that we were up late fucking?"

Lira giggled. "No, but...what *are* we going to tell her?"

"Nothing yet. No one needs to know anything yet."

Lira tilted her head. "Why not? Are you embarrassed?"

"Embarrassed? That the prettiest girl in Brookwood is my..."

"Your what, Amy?"

Amy threw her hands up. "I don't know, Lira. What are you?"

Lira looked down, stepping into her skirt. "I guess I don't know either. Am I your girlfriend now?"

"Do you want to be?"

"Only if you want me to be."

"Fine, then, you're my girlfriend. So I snagged the prettiest girl in Brookwood, probably the prettiest in the Midwest, and maybe even the prettiest in the world. No, I'm not embarrassed. But our relationship just underwent a major and very sudden change. I think we need time to process it ourselves before we tell everyone we know."

"I suppose you have a point." Lira followed Amy to the kitchen and began pouring herself a bowl of cereal while Amy started the coffee.

"Here's the thing," said Amy. "If I had slept with anyone else for the first time ever last night, I would have called you this morning and told you all about it. And you would be the only person I told today, maybe even this week. I would wait to see what happened next. But last night it was you that I slept with, and I kind of still only want to tell you about it."

Lira smiled. "I understand."

Amy turned and put her hands on Lira's shoulders. "You know once we tell my family and everyone at work that we're together, they're going to be part of our relationship too. I want it to be just us for a little while."

Lira hugged her and planted a kiss on her lips. "We can do that."

Amy smiled at her. "I doubt we can keep it a secret too long. But maybe I can have time to gather my thoughts before I deal with my mom."

"Do you think she'll react badly?"

"I don't know," said Amy, her brow furrowed. "She's not extremely homophobic, but I've always gotten the impression she would be disappointed if one of her own children was gay. I think she'd come around though, if she knew I was happy. And she does love you."

"Are you?"

"Am I what? Happy, or gay?"

"Both."

Amy's face softened. "What we did last night made me extremely happy. The idea of being allowed to love you, the way I already love you but not secretly anymore, makes me ecstatic. And if that means I'm gay, then so be it."

"It doesn't necessarily mean you're gay. It could mean you're bi."

"Maybe. But no guy ever did for me what you did last night. Hell, no guy's ever done for me what you do just by looking at me. You're kind of more amazing than anybody."

Lira grinned. "Well, it doesn't matter to me what your sexual orientation is as long as you want to be with me."

"No worries there. So, how are you feeling today? Better about stuff?"

"You mean my mom?"

Amy nodded.

"Well, I'm distracted for now. It's still something I have to deal with. But you definitely succeeded in taking my mind off of it."

Amy frowned. "So, for you, how much is this about…taking your mind off things?"

"Oh, Amy." Lira kissed her again. "None of it. This is what I want. This is sort of what I've always wanted, I think. I just didn't always realize it."

"Really?" Amy's face lit up. "Because I think I've been kind of in love with you practically since I met you."

"*Amy!* Why didn't you say something a lot sooner? We could be married by now!"

"Well that escalated quickly," said Amy, raising her eyebrows. "I didn't tell you sooner because I didn't think you would ever feel the same way. I just hoped I'd get over it."

"Well I'm glad you finally got up the nerve to do something about it."

"*You* could have said something too."

"I'd never had such a close friend before. I thought maybe this was just how it felt."

"Oh, Lira." Amy turned back to the coffee maker. "I meant what I said, last night. Next time you're having a bad day, I want you to remember that there is at least one person in the world who loves you more than anything, no matter what."

Lira accepted the cup of coffee Amy offered, beaming. "I don't think I'll forget."

Chapter 6

Amy was glad most of the people she worked with were men. Not one of them noticed her moodiness that day, as she agonized over whether she and Lira were doing the right thing. She'd spend about an hour feeling like the luckiest and happiest human being on the planet, then spend another hour hating herself for dragging Lira into this ill-advised relationship that would probably ruin both their lives, then go back to feeling happy again. She and Luis spent most of the day interviewing people who knew Jennifer O'Malley, so it was late afternoon before she had the chance to make an excuse to head over to the morgue and see Lira.

She was happy to see that Lira was alone in her office when she found her. After glancing around to make sure no one was nearby, Amy took Lira in her arms and kissed her.

"We probably shouldn't do that at work," said Lira, but she was smiling.

"Do what?" asked Amy, eyes wide with mock innocence.

Lira giggled. "So how did the interviews go?"

"Okay I guess, but we still haven't found any connection whatsoever between Jennifer O'Malley and Kelly Bruin. The only thing they have in common is age, hair color, and body type. My gut feeling says this guy is serial, or at least he plans to be. He just hasn't killed enough people yet for it to be official."

"Well, hopefully we can stop him before he kills anyone else, so he'll never be serial."

"I hope so, but so far we have nothing. *Nothing* useful. The DNA is worthless if we don't have anything to connect it to. And while we're here spinning our wheels, Jennifer O'Malley is probably going through hell. I hate this case. I *hate* it." She ran her fingers through her hair in frustration, hit a bunch of tangles, pulled them back out. "The worst part is that it's happening *right now*. If we're right that Jennifer was taken by the same person as Kelly was, then she's somewhere out there right now, getting drugged, violently raped, and having weird tally marks carved into her skin. And we can't do a damn thing about it." She froze and looked down at Lira. "Wait a minute, that's it, isn't it? That was what you didn't want to say?"

"What is?"

"The tally marks. It's the number of times he's raping her, isn't it?"

Lira frowned. "Well, that *is* what I thought, but it's just one theory. There's no evidence to support it. It could be something else entirely."

Amy sighed. "Well, I guess you're right that it doesn't really bring us any closer to catching him. It just makes me hate him more."

Lira took Amy's hand. "When I leave here, I'm going to go home and cook us dinner. I can make it like an official date, if you want. I'll light candles. It'll take your mind off the case."

"I've never understood why candlelight dinners are supposed to be so romantic. How is hardly being able to see you going to help me feel more attracted to you?"

Lira laughed. "Actually, dining by candlelight forces you to focus on the person in front of you by blocking out your surroundings. Also, the dim lighting causes your pupils to dilate, which is also a sign of attraction, and it's always a turn on to see someone who appears to be attracted to you."

"Duly noted. Well, you can get out the candles if you want, but…" She glanced around and then lowered her voice. "You already know I'm attracted to you, and I'm not going to be looking anywhere else."

Lira tilted her head. "Interesting."

"What's interesting?"

"I always thought your pupils were slightly larger than average, but if you think about it, I only see your pupils when you're looking at *me*. You could have been showing signs of attraction all along and I just didn't realize."

"I don't believe it," said Amy. "The brilliant Dr. Ward overlooked an important clue."

***

When Amy left work that evening, the first place she went

was to a bookstore. She wandered around for a few minutes, eventually finding some books about sex, but they all seemed to be for straight couples. *I learned how to do that without a manual*, she thought. She considered just leaving and resolving to keep winging it, but she decided Lira deserved better. She went on the hunt for an employee, but the first one she found was a guy, so she quickly backtracked until she found a female employee.

"Can I help you?" the lady asked.

"Yes, um, do you have any..." She looked around nervously, leaned very close to the employee, and said, in her lowest audible voice, "...any kind of manuals or something for, um, you know, lesbian sex?" She cringed as soon as the words were out of her mouth.

The lady smiled. "Right this way," she said. She led Amy to the LGBT section (*damn it, why didn't I think to look there?* Amy thought) and showed her a few guides to lesbian sex. Amy decided to buy one of each, just to be safe, although she was extremely embarrassed when she checked out. She headed out to her car and stuffed the books under the back seat. *Of course, she's going to expect me to do it again before I get the chance to read the damn books*, she thought, but it couldn't be helped.

As she drove to Lira's, all she could think about was how badly she'd fucked up by kissing her in the first place. She'd just wanted to make her feel better, but why didn't she just hug her like usual, or give her a kiss on the cheek? Now she felt like she'd signed a contract to keep Lira happy for the rest of her life. She couldn't just back out. Lira would be hurt. But if Amy failed her somewhere down the line, she would be hurt even worse. Their friendship was the best thing Amy had in her life, and now she had wrecked it.

Amy parked her car at Lira's and walked into a dark house. Lira had indeed set candles up on the dining table and was busy in the kitchen, her big fluffy cat meowing at her feet.

"Hello Amy!" she said cheerfully. "Dinner's almost ready! I'm making oricchiette bolognese."

Amy didn't know what the hell that was, but she figured she'd find out when she ate it. She sat down at the table and realized she should have thought to stop somewhere other than the bookstore.

"I'm sorry," she said. "I'm a horrible date. I should have brought you flowers or a bottle of wine or something. I just don't know how to do this."

"It's okay!" Lira assured her. "I have a 2004 Chianti Superiore for us. I only needed you to bring yourself." She brought the food to the table and began pouring the wine. "This date's on me, but you can do the next one, if you want."

"Oh, yeah. You can come to my place and I'll make you a grilled cheese sandwich, paired with a nice beer."

Lira smiled and sat down across from Amy. "You know I wouldn't mind if you did. We'd still have fun."

Amy made a face. "I'm starting to think all you care about is seeing me naked."

"That *is* one of the things I want." Lira's smile faltered. "Is something bothering you?"

"I just…I feel like I've lost my best friend."

Lira frowned. "But I'm right here."

"I know, but…yesterday you were my best friend, and today you're my girlfriend."

Lira put her hand on Amy's. "I'm still your best friend. I'll always be your best friend. I can be two things at once."

"But what if we don't work out as a couple? We'll lose everything."

"No we won't. Amy, we've been friends for three years. We've gone through a lot together. There's no reason why this would ruin it. I think we'll work out, but if we don't, we can still be best friends."

"That's what everyone says, and then it doesn't happen."

"Most people weren't BFFs for years before they got together. You're the most important person in my life, Amy. I'm not going to give you up that easily."

Amy smiled slightly. "I hope not. I really do want this to work."

"We already know each other really well. I think we have an

excellent chance."

Amy sipped her wine. "So, am I supposed to cut off all my hair and go full butch now?"

Lira's eyes shot daggers at her. "If you cut off your hair, I will break up with you."

"So you only want me for my hair?"

"I want you for *you*. Amy, I don't want you to change anything about yourself for me. *You* are the person I fell in love with. I want you to stay exactly the way you are. Also, I love your hair."

"Okay, okay. This is just uncharted territory for me."

"It is for me too, but I know it isn't going to work if we try to fit into some stereotype. Let's just be us, together."

"I can do that." Amy ate quietly for a minute, feeling a little ashamed. Maybe she *was* making too much of things. "You know, with this candlelight, I can't even see what color your eyes are."

"Don't you know what color my eyes are?"

"Of course, but…" She looked down. "They're pretty. And I can't see them."

Lira broke into a grin that made Amy's anxiety dissipate. "I'll turn the lights back on as soon as we're done eating."

***

Becky Sadler often drove by her daughter's best friend's house on her way to and from her own house, which was just half a mile up the road. She sometimes stopped in to say hello, because Lira was such a sweetheart, and she had to get lonely living all by herself with no family nearby. The only family the poor girl really had was a weird mother who never came to see her, and Becky couldn't imagine why. She would be thrilled to have a daughter like Lira. Of course, Amy was wonderful too, and that was another reason for popping by Lira's house from time to time: as often as not, Amy was there. So she wasn't very surprised to see Amy's car out front when she came by after her book club meeting to drop off a novel she was finished with and just knew Lira would love. She could see a light on in the big bay window of the dining room (oh, it was such a gorgeous old house, and Lira was so proud of it) as she walked up onto the porch with the book. As she reached for the doorbell, she glanced through the leaded glass of the dining room window and froze.

Amy and Lira were in there clearing away what looked almost like the remains of a romantic dinner. She could see a bottle of wine, candles, Lira's nice dishes. Amy was holding two stacked plates and saying something to Lira, who smiled adoringly in response and reached up to run her fingers through Amy's curls. There was something familiar about the gesture, as though she had done it before, and yet there was something reverent about it as well. In response, Amy leaned forward and kissed Lira's face, ever so gently, as though Lira were the most precious thing in the world.

"They must think I was born yesterday," Becky muttered as she turned around and headed back to her car.

Chapter 7

"Mmm. I could get used to waking up like this."

Lira smiled at Amy's first words of the morning. It was early, and they were tangled together in Lira's bed. Lira hoped they would wake up like this many, many more times, hopefully for the rest of their lives. "I think it'll take me a while to get used to this," she said, planting a kiss on Amy's bare shoulder. "It's hard to get used to something this amazing."

"It *is* pretty fucking amazing." Amy toyed with Lira's hair. "So, someone's touching the back of my head, but you're in front of me."

Lira giggled. "It's the cat. She likes the smell of your hair." Clea was alternating between sniffing Amy's hair and blissfully rubbing her head against it.

"Ah." Amy reached back and awkwardly petted the cat. "I told you I'd get her to like me. But that reminds me. I need to go home and walk Henry."

"Maybe you should bring him with you next time. I could start keeping some dog food here. He and Clea got along when you brought him over before."

"Yeah, I'll think about it." Amy grabbed her phone from the night stand. "Damn it, why does my mom always have to text me first thing in the morning when I'm busy being naked with you? She wants us to meet her for breakfast."

"That would be lovely."

"I'm not so sure. She's up to something."

"Oh, Amy. You should be grateful to have a mother who wants to spend time with you."

"You wanna trade?"

"No. But I think we should have breakfast with your mom."

"Fine." Amy heaved herself from the bed and stumbled to the bathroom.

When they were both dressed and the dog had been walked and fed, they headed to the diner Becky wanted to meet them at. They found her waiting for them outside, and as always, Lira felt comforted by the mere sight of the maternal woman. Becky had warm, dark skin, chin-length hair that she always kept neatly curled, and wire-rimmed glasses. Her face was round where Amy's was angular, and she always had a pleasant, open expression. She greeted them both with warm hugs, to Lira's delighted surprise.

"Lira, I had my book club last night, and the next book we're reading is your mom's latest!" Becky gushed. "No one can believe I know Genevieve Ward's daughter! They all want to know what you're like and I told them you're just the sweetest thing. Which you are," she added, suddenly looking serious. "And we already consider you to be part of the Sadler family."

"Thank you," said Lira, a bit puzzled.

"So," said Becky as the three of them sat down, "what's new with you girls?"

"Not much," said Amy quickly. "I'm just, you know, solving crimes and stuff. Lira's been busy cutting up dead bodies. The usual."

"I always forget that you do that," Becky said to Lira. "It amazes me that someone with your delightful personality can spend her days with dead people. How do you do it?"

"It doesn't really bother me," Lira assured her. "Working with death has only made me appreciate life more. I know how quickly it can be taken away."

"That's a really good way of looking at it!" agreed Becky. "Life is much too short not to tell the people you love important things." She looked meaningfully between the two younger women, who looked uncertainly at each other.

"Life's definitely too short not to order the Everything Pancake," concluded Amy, picking up her menu. "Five fruit toppings plus ice cream and chocolate syrup! Now *that* is what I call breakfast."

"Your life *will* be shorter if you eat that sort of thing for breakfast on a regular basis," Lira laughed.

The rest of the breakfast conversation was nothing out of the ordinary, until they all got ready to leave and Becky pulled them into a group hug.

"I just want you both to know that this family supports you

no matter what," she said earnestly.

"What the hell has gotten into you?" asked Amy. "Support us in what?"

"In everything. Amy, I will always love you, and there's nothing that will change that. You'll always be my precious little girl."

"Gross," said Amy, wrenching herself away. "I'm gonna go pay our bill."

Becky turned to Lira. "You know how much we all love you, right, Lira?"

"Y-yes. Why?"

"I just want you to know. And, if it were anyone else, I might be upset. But since it's you, I'm going to try and keep an open mind."

Lira exchanged a look with Amy as they walked out of the diner, but they couldn't say anything yet. Amy noticed her phone buzzing and took it out.

"That's odd," she said. "Captain Wheeler says there's a new piece of evidence in the tally marks case. He wants me to see it before he sends it to the lab."

"I have a few minutes before my shift starts. Do you think he'll mind if I come see it?" Lira asked.

"I'll ask him," said Amy, typing on her phone. "What the fuck, now my sister is texting that she's there if I need to talk. What the hell is wrong with people today?"

"I think that's a very nice text to get from your sister."

"Well, you don't have one, so you don't know how weird it is. Okay, Wheeler says it's fine if I bring you."

Lira knew she was the only person from the Coroner's Office to regularly visit the Homicide Unit, but no one seemed to bat an eye when she showed up. On their arrival they found Captain Wheeler, the head of Homicide, a seasoned cop in his late fifties. He had a perpetual grizzled stubble and a gruff attitude, but he tended to be fatherly towards the younger detectives like Amy and Luis. Although he ran the department, he only got personally involved in the most serious cases.

"Look what came in the mail yesterday," he said, showing Amy and Lira a small evidence bag. Inside was a photograph of Kelly Bruin, asleep in a single bed with an iron headboard. She appeared to be naked under a plain white blanket. On her shoulders they could see some of the tally marks she'd been found with.

"Our unsub sent that?" asked Amy. "Is he nuts?"

"Look at the back," said Wheeler. He flipped the bag over and they could see that the back of the photograph was covered in tally marks, drawn in red ink.

"Let me see that," said Lira, grabbing the bag. She studied the back of the picture carefully. "Two hundred seventy-one marks. The same number that was on Kelly's body."

"So basically, he's taunting us," said Amy. "Did he send this to anyone in particular?"

"It was just addressed to the Brookwood Police Department. That's why I didn't see it until just now, but I told them to let us know right away if anything similar shows up. I'm hoping the lab can process it and tell us if there's anything traceable. Fingerprints, an unusual kind of ink, anything."

"Let's hope so," agreed Amy.

***

Lira spent her morning doing an autopsy on a drowning victim. At lunchtime, Amy came to the morgue and dropped an evidence bag on Lira's desk.

"Guess what came in the mail today," she said grimly.

Lira picked up the bag and saw a photograph of Jennifer O'Malley, lying on the same bed Kelly had been in. Unlike Kelly, she was awake in her picture; her eyes were filled with pure terror. Lira flipped the picture over. On the back were five tally marks, and scrawled under them were the words *SO FAR*.

"I think you were right about the marks," said Amy quietly.

Tears welled up in Lira's eyes. "This is terrible!" she exclaimed. "This is even sicker than what we normally see!"

"I know. And seeing this picture of Jennifer only makes it that much more real." Amy sighed. "I hate this guy, Lira. I *hate* him."

"I hope you can find her soon and get her out of there. She looks so scared." She handed the picture back. "I wish there was more I could do to help."

"I know, Lira. We're all doing everything we can. We met with a few detectives from the Sex Crimes Unit this morning, including Mitch which I wasn't too happy about, but I sucked it up because a woman's life is on the line. We need all hands on deck right now. Anyway, I just need to run this by the lab and then we can go get something to eat. There weren't any prints on the first one, but maybe this one will be different."

"Okay," said Lira, reaching for her jacket.

"So, I'm pretty sure my mom and sister know about us, and now my brother is texting too. You didn't say anything, did you?"

"No, I haven't said anything. You didn't, did you?"

"No. I don't know how they figured it out, but they know."

"Maybe your mom saw your car at my house last night or this morning, and it made her suspicious."

"It's hardly the first time I've spent the night at your house."

"No, but she also knows *I* spent the night with *you* the night before last. That's a lot of togetherness even for us."

"Maybe we *are* being too obvious." Amy shrugged. "You know what? I don't even give a shit anymore. If they put it together, they put it together. I've got much bigger things to worry about than whether people know I'm sleeping with you."

Lira smiled.

Chapter 8

By the time two months had passed, Amy and Lira had long since told nearly everyone about their relationship. They had gotten mixed reactions at first, but all the surprise and uncertainty had long since died down. Everyone was used to the situation now, and really, it was surprising how little had changed. They had settled into a comfortable routine and gained a lot of confidence in bed, and most of Amy's relationship fears had gone away. She felt like she was doing what she had always been meant to do. She was just thinking she couldn't ever remember being this happy before when Jennifer O'Malley's body turned up.

It was a different dumpster this time, in a different part of town, but she was disposed of in the same way Kelly had been: completely naked, with tally marks carved into her skin. Amy and Luis had the unpleasant task of going to inform her parents that she had been found dead and watching them implode the way Mark Bruin had done. This was twice now for the same killer

"One hundred sixty-eight tally marks this time," Lira announced when Amy came to see how the autopsy was going the next day. "Not as many, but he didn't keep her as long."

"I wonder why not," said Amy.

"He might have planned to longer. Her cause of death isn't the same as Kelly's."

"Well she doesn't have the bruising around her throat. How did she die?"

"Respiratory failure. Of course we don't have toxicology results yet, but I'm wondering if he accidentally gave her too much ketamine. It can depress breathing at higher doses, which is why breathing is always monitored closely when it's administered in a surgical setting. Possibly he tried to give her enough to keep her out a little longer, and she simply stopped breathing. Her sternum is fractured, which implies that he attempted CPR."

"Wow, he must have been pissed if she died before she was supposed to. When perps strangle victims with their bare hands, it's usually because they like the feeling of life leaving the person's body. Everything we've seen from him so far implies that he likes being in control of his victims. I'd hate to see how he reacted when she just died. Now he's going to be in a hurry to find another one."

Lira nodded her agreement. "She has mostly the same injuries as Kelly had. Bite marks on her breasts, needle marks in her arm, tearing and bruising in her vagina. It looks like he slapped the right side of her face pretty hard, which means he's probably left-handed. She also has a partially healed fracture of her fifth rib, which wouldn't be from the CPR."

"Maybe he had to work a little harder to subdue this one," Amy suggested hopefully. She wanted someone to fight him, to make things just a little more difficult for him.

Lira looked troubled. "Amy, I want you to move in with me."

Amy's eyes nearly popped out of her head. "Lira! I hardly think this is the time to discuss something like that!"

"I think this is exactly the time, Amy. Look at this woman. She never expected to be abducted, tortured, and murdered. None of us knows when we might lose everything. Life is too short for us to put things off. I want you with me all the time. I want us to make a life together, and I want to start now."

"But we've only been dating two months."

"If we'd only met two months ago, I would say you had a point, but we've been practically in a relationship for years. I'm not asking you to *marry* me. I just want you to live with me. You spend most of your time at my house anyway."

"I do, but…then I'd be near my mom and she would drive by and spy on me, like she already does to you."

"How much more often would she really be 'spying' on you if you lived at my house, as opposed to just spending the night four or five times a week?"

"Well, I guess not much more…"

"And we wouldn't have to stay in that house forever. Someday we could buy a big old house by the river and fix it up, and it would really be *our* house. But for now, I just want you with me. We waited too long to get together in the first place. I don't want to wait too long again." Her voice broke.

"Lira, come here." Amy walked around the autopsy table and pulled Lira into her arms, which was a little awkward since they were both in full autopsy gear, but she would make it work. Lira pressed her face to Amy's chest, and Amy rubbed her back. "We won't wait too long about anything else," she promised. "Remember what I told you when we got together? I love you. I love *everything* about you. I love you more than anything." She kissed Lira's head. "And I have always been putty in your hands, so I don't know what you're worried about. You always get your way with me in the end."

Lira laughed through her tears. "Not always."

"Almost always. So cheer up. Just give me a little time to think about it, okay?"

"Of course. I don't want you making a hasty decision. Especially not over a dead body." She pulled back. "I'm sorry. I just got emotional. I was really hoping we would find her alive."

"Yeah, we all were."

Amy returned to the station to do some paperwork related to the case, then came back to grab Lira for a late lunch. Lira was a little cheerier by then, but Amy could tell the stress of the case was still wearing on her. She couldn't blame her; knowing another woman could be kidnapped any day by the same sicko was wearing her down as well.

"Do you have a whole hour for lunch today?" Lira asked her.

"Yeah, unless I get a call saying otherwise."

Lira nodded. "I always lock the door to my office when I leave for lunch."

"That's…smart, but why are you telling me this?"

"Because if we eat fast enough, I might have time to sneak you back to my office, lock the door, and give you an orgasm on my couch while everyone thinks we're still at lunch."

Amy's eyes widened. "So, not only do you want to have sex at work, but *I* get to have the orgasm? Are you still thinking about how short life is, or is this part of your campaign to get me to move in with you?"

"Mostly the former, but you did give me one this morning, and there wasn't enough time for me to do you. It makes me feel unbalanced." She smiled brightly. "So now I want to hit that!"

Amy nearly spit out her drink. "Lira, please, it's better if you don't try to sound hip," she said, but she couldn't stop laughing. "You know what? I think I've eaten enough. Shall we do our sneaking around?"

Lira grinned and jumped up from the table. Amy paid the bill and followed her back to the morgue and into her office, where Lira quickly locked the door and checked the blinds.

"I think I like this side of you," said Amy. "The rebellious, rule-breaking side."

Lira flashed her a smile. "Get on the couch."

Amy got on the couch. "Now your bossy side I was already familiar with. Most people don't realize you have that side."

"I mostly only show it to you," admitted Lira, swiftly removing Amy's shirt and bra. She sucked each of Amy's nipples in turn, blowing on each one afterwards, which always made Amy squirm in the best possible way. Then Lira finished undressing her and began deftly working her clit with her fingers. Amy glanced up at the window that looked out into the hallway to make absolutely sure the blinds were properly closed. They were, so she relaxed and let herself enjoy Lira's incredible fine motor skills. Lira had often remarked that she loved Amy's long fingers, but Amy decided shorter fingers were just fine as long as you knew what to do with them. And Lira did.

Amy closed her eyes as Lira easily found her G-spot. There were definite advantages to having a girlfriend who was intimately familiar with human anatomy. As Lira brought her to climax, she grabbed the couch cushions and bit her lip to try to keep from crying out. Lira took her into her arms and kissed her.

"I love you so much," Lira whispered.

"I love you too, and I don't want to rush you, but I'm expected next door in five minutes."

Lira let go of Amy and watched her get dressed. "I feel more balanced now," she observed.

"That's great." Amy fastened on her gun holster and her badge. "Do I look like someone just fucked me on a couch?"

Lira smiled enigmatically.

"I mean it, Lira, you can't let me go next door looking like we just did what we did. If the guys figure it out, they'll never let me live it down."

Lira stood and smoothed out Amy's clothes and hair. "You look ready to catch bad guys," she assured her.

"Good." She gave Lira one last kiss before hurrying outside.

Chapter 9

When Lira got the text from Amy a few days later, she hurried next door as quickly as she could. She desperately hoped it would be a break in the case that had been stressing them all out for over two months, but when she arrived in Homicide, she found everyone looking pretty depressed.

"We got a picture of Jennifer today," said Amy, "and we have another missing woman."

Lira took the picture from Amy. It was what appeared to be a more recent photograph of Jennifer O'Malley: she looked thinner than in her previous picture, and her eyes now had a listless appearance instead of the abject terror from before. On the back were one hundred and sixty-eight red tally marks.

"Our new missing woman is Rebecca Laurent," said Captain Wheeler, motioning towards the screen in front of him. There was a picture of another woman with reddish hair and a similar build to the previous two. "She's thirty-seven years old," Wheeler continued. "Her husband says she usually beats him home from work. He got home last night, her car was there, but she wasn't. He found her keys and purse next to the car. Looks like he took her just as she was getting out."

"He doesn't have much of a cooling-off period," said Luis. "My thinking is that he already has his next victim picked out before he kills the one he has."

"Jennifer died before he was ready, though," Amy pointed out.

Luis shrugged. "Maybe he picks the next one way in advance. He's picking women with a similar appearance and stalking them so he knows when and where he can take them without being seen. A day or two before he plans to take her, he kills the one he's already got and tosses the body behind a dumpster. What we don't know is what makes him suddenly want a new one."

"Maybe he gets sick of them after they're all carved up," said Amy bitterly.

"Or maybe the thrill of the abduction is a big part of it for him," suggested Wheeler.

Lira noticed Amy blinking back tears as she looked at the picture of Jennifer O'Malley. "What is it?"

Amy swiped at her eye with the back of her hand. "I just noticed that she looks a little like you." She looked up at Lira. "It just made me think. If anything like that happened to you…"

"I understand." Lira leaned forward and whispered mischievously, "I'd feel pretty safe if I had a cop living with me, though."

Amy laughed. "Be careful what you wish for. I called my landlord this morning. They're gonna find someone to sublet my apartment. I told them I'd move my stuff out this weekend."

Lira broke into a grin. "Really?"

"Yes, really. So don't make me regret it!"

Chapter 10

Amy spent the weekend moving her things to Lira's house, with the help of friends and family. In some ways it felt a little abrupt, but once she'd made the decision, it seemed pointless to wait. She *did* spend most of her time at Lira's, and she'd known from the start that she wanted to be in this for the long haul. She wouldn't have risked their friendship if she hadn't thought they could make this a lifelong thing.

As for Lira, she was positively ecstatic to have Amy officially in her house – or *their* house, as she now insisted on calling it. Becky also seemed pleased that her daughter was finally settling down with someone. She came by Sunday night, after everyone else who had helped with the move had gone home, and gave them a potted plant as a housewarming present.

"Mom, you know Lira's lived here for a while," Amy pointed out as Lira happily read the little card that came with the plant to determine what kind of sunlight it needed so she could find the perfect spot.

"Yes, but it's a new beginning for both of you, and I want you both to know how happy I am for you," gushed Becky. "I never thought my Amy was going to meet the right person and settle down, but it turns out she was just looking in the wrong place. She didn't need the right *man*; she needed the right woman!"

Lira giggled. "Well, I hope I am that for her."

"You certainly are, my dear. And maybe someday you two can think about giving me grandkids?"

"Mom! That's completely inappropriate!" chided Amy. "We've only been dating for two months!"

"Oh, honey, nobody believes that. I get it, you were afraid of how people would react. Nobody's mad at you for keeping it a secret so long. We just don't understand why you feel the need to lie to us now about how long you've been together!"

Amy and Lira looked at each other. "Becky, we started dating two months ago," Lira assured her. "You saw us together on our first official date. Then we told everyone."

Becky looked perplexed. "But you two have acted like a couple for so long. I thought I was blind not to see it sooner."

"Well, Mom, you weren't the only blind one," said Amy. "We really did wait that long to get together."

When Becky finally left, Lira got out a bottle of wine, chuckling softly. "I'm glad your mom is so supportive."

"What did yours say when you told her I was moving in?"

Lira sighed. "That she was happy for me."

"That's good. She's still not bothered by the gay stuff?"

"No, that's never bothered her. She's not crazy about cops though."

"It's always something, isn't it?" Amy accepted the glass of wine Lira had poured for her. "My mom's not going to stop bugging us about grandkids now."

"Have you told her you don't want kids?"

"No, I never decided that."

Lira looked at her contemplatively. "So that's something you would be open to discussing at some point?"

"Yeah, sure, if you wanted to."

Lira smiled. "Not anytime soon, but I might want to. Discuss it. Someday."

Amy took Lira's hand, pulled her closer, and kissed her. "I'm up for just about any kind of discussion with you, my beautiful girl."

Lira sighed happily.

***

On Monday, they received a picture of Rebecca Laurent in the mail. There were three tally marks on the back.

Four months later, they found her body behind a dumpster.

Amy was numb with frustration. Their unsub was officially a serial killer now, and they still had no tangible leads. Wheeler was considering calling in the FBI.

"How many tally marks this time?" she asked while Lira was typing up the autopsy report. Her voice was utterly devoid of emotion.

"Three hundred fourteen. Cause of death is manual

strangulation, so it looks like she died on schedule. Same injuries as the other two." She looked up at Amy. "She was also five weeks pregnant."

"Five weeks? So it had to be his."

"And he's probably already picked out whom he's taking next, hasn't he?"

Amy sighed and rubbed her forehead. "Most likely. I'm sure we'll be getting a picture of *her* before long."

Lira hesitated. "I wish—"

"We both wish, Lira. We all do."

Lira nodded and turned back to her computer. Amy went back to the station, feeling depressed. Three women dead, two on her watch, and no leads. When was this going to end?

Chapter 11

When they got home that evening, Lira poured two glasses of wine and curled up on the couch with Amy. Amy had a ball game on, which was of no real interest to Lira, but she was glad Amy had found something to focus on besides the depressing case. She pulled the blanket over their laps and leaned her head on Amy's shoulder. Amy put an arm around her and kissed the top of her head.

"I'm glad you live here now," said Lira. "I like knowing you'll always be here at the end of a long day."

Amy smiled at her. "Me too." She sipped her wine. "You know what? You are, hands down, the best thing about my life. You make all the shitty stuff worthwhile."

"So do you." Lira lifted her face and kissed Amy's lips. "You know, I love everything about you."

"Mmm. I will bring that up next time you're mad at me."

Lira smiled and touched Amy's hand on her shoulder, lacing their fingers together. "Can you believe we've been together six months already? And we've lived together four of those months."

Amy thought for a moment. "It does seem weird, doesn't it? Sometimes I still can't believe I'm actually allowed to kiss you."

"It was the best thing you ever did. Kissing me, I mean, that first time. That was what set everything in motion. I've been happier with you than I've ever been before in my life."

"Me too." Amy finished her wine and wrapped both arms tightly around Lira. "You sure know how to get me out of a bad mood."

Lira set her glass down. "You know what would decrease our stress even more?"

"Orgasms?"

Lira giggled. "You know me so well." She got up and took Amy's hand, pulling her from the couch and leading her up to the bedroom. Once there, she slid her arms around Amy and kissed her gently, slowly, wanting to make her completely relaxed. She moved her lips and tongue along Amy's jawline and down her neck. Amy's body had become intimately familiar to her over the last six months, and she found she loved every little detail more and more as time passed. She hoped this was where she would always be: here, in Amy's arms.

"Is it bad that I want sex after working on a horrifying case all day?" Amy asked her. "I'm not gonna develop some weird association, am I?"

Lira laughed gently. "It would only be a problem if you reached a point where you were unable to get aroused without working on a disturbing case first."

"Well I don't think *that's* gonna happen. Being with you is what gets me aroused, and I'm pretty sure it always will."

"I certainly hope so." Lira kissed her again. "It's very healthy to be able to unwind and enjoy intimacy with your partner after a stressful day, and the endorphins released during sex are great stress relievers. Plus, our relationship shouldn't suffer just because of the case you're working on."

"I'd never let that happen." Amy carefully lowered Lira onto the bed, covering her face with reverent kisses. "I love you," she said quietly, unzipping Lira's dress and easing it off of her. "I love everything about you." She gently caressed Lira's arms, her sides, before unhooking her bra and sliding it off. "I love you more than anything." Lira closed her eyes and reveled in the feeling of the kisses raining down on her shoulders, chest, breasts. She had never felt so loved, so cherished as she did with Amy. She had never had someone love everything about her before.

Three hours later, both women were wrapped in each other's arms, completely sated. Lira held Amy close and drifted into a peaceful slumber, feeling the warmth and security of Amy's love wrapped around her.

She hoped she would never fall asleep any other way again.

MICHELLE ARNOLD

Chapter 12

Amy could barely focus at work the next day. She was tired because she and Lira had spent a few hours "relieving each other's stress" the night before, and also distracted because that "stress relief" had been *amazing*. When she first got to work, she just slumped at her desk and stared at the picture of Lira she had taped to her computer monitor, until Luis snapped her out of it. He had noticed her staring dreamily at Lira's picture and was snickering at his desk, so Amy wadded up a piece of paper and threw it at him.

"Stop fighting, kids. You have a shooting to investigate," said Wheeler sternly as he passed by on the way to his office, but Amy could tell he was amused.

The shooting had taken place the day before and was the sort of domestic dispute they saw all the time. It wouldn't take long to solve. In a way, it was nice to have such a standard case to focus on for the day instead of agonizing over their sadistic serial killer, but interviewing witnesses took until mid-afternoon, so Amy wasn't able to have lunch with Lira. When they finally got back, she planned to go over to the morgue to get a glimpse of her beautiful girlfriend, but Clarissa, the resident currently working with Lira, surprised her in the police station lobby.

"Detective Sadler," she said nervously, "have you heard from Dr. Ward? She said she was going by her – your house on her lunch break, but she never came back, and she's not answering her phone. Has she been with you?"

Amy could feel her entire world crashing down around her. Without a word, she turned around and ran back out to her car.

She tried Lira's phone several times on the drive home, but it just rang and rang and then went to voicemail. She turned on her siren, only turning it off when she reached the block where they lived. Lira's car was there. *That means she's home*, she thought absurdly, even though she knew perfectly well that Lira would never just go home for lunch and stay there. She went in the front door and called Lira's name, but only Henry and Clea were there to greet her. Amy walked quickly around the house, her heart thudding in her chest. Everything was exactly the way she had left it that morning. There was the living room couch, where they had been cuddled up drinking wine just last night; and the kitchen, with their breakfast dishes still in the sink; and the dining room, where they enjoyed both intimate meals for two and noisy Sadler family gatherings.

Maybe she's upstairs, thought Amy. *Maybe she was really tired and she decided to lie down for a bit, and she just zonked out. She'll be so horrified when I wake her up and she sees what time it is.*

But their bed was still neatly made with those purple satin sheets Lira liked. The bathroom was empty, and the spare bedroom Lira used as her library. Amy went back downstairs and tried Lira's phone again. This time she heard a very faint buzzing. She followed the sound to the back door and slowly opened it, already knowing what she would find.

Lira's purse, phone, and keys were lying on the ground outside the back door.

And Lira was gone.

Chapter 13

When Luis and Wheeler arrived, they found Amy still kneeling next to Lira's things.

"She's gone," she said hoarsely when she saw them. "He took her. He *took her*." She looked up and made eye contact with Luis. "We're never going to find her, are we?"

"Don't say that," said Luis sharply. "We'll find her. Of course we will."

"We worked so hard to find the others, and we couldn't. He's too good."

"We're going to find her," insisted Luis. "He'll make a mistake soon." He knelt down next to his partner and put his arm around her. She leaned against him and started sobbing.

"I can't live without her, Luis. I can't."

"You won't have to." Luis looked helplessly at Wheeler, but his expression was not reassuring. "Right, I'm going to do what Lira would do. I'm taking you inside and making you a cup of tea."

"Good idea," Wheeler agreed. "Maybe then we can talk some more and figure out where to go next."

"I don't want any tea," Amy insisted as Luis helped her to her feet. "We don't have time for tea. We have to try to find her before he hurts her."

The two men gave her that helpless look again.

"Lira needs you to be able to think clearly," Luis insisted, leading everyone inside. "You know if she were here she would make you a cup of hot tea to calm your nerves, so that's what I'm going to do." He searched through the kitchen while Amy slumped into a counter chair, head in her hands.

"He's been taunting us for a while," said Wheeler. "Maybe he didn't take her for the same reason he took the others. Maybe he took one of our own because he wants something from us."

"That could be," said Luis hopefully, putting the kettle on the stove. "If that's the case, he might not hurt her the way he did the others."

Amy peered at them over her fingers. "I wish I could believe that," she said, "but she's his type. She's the right age, right body type, right hair color. This is the kind of woman he goes for. He might have zeroed in on her to taunt us further, but if he just wanted someone for ransom or something, why not take me or one of the other cops? Why take a forensic pathologist, who happens to resemble the other women?" She sighed. "I want you guys to be right. I do. But my gut says he took her because he wants her. And we all know what that means he's going to do to her."

The men shifted uncomfortably, knowing she was right.

"I'll go interview the neighbors, see if anyone saw anything," said Wheeler. "When I'm done, we'll all go back to the station."

He went out the back door. Luis put a cup of tea in front of Amy.

"Please drink this," he said. "For Lira."

Amy bitterly sipped at the tea, but her hands were shaking so hard she could barely hold the cup. It tasted horrible, nothing like what Lira made. Unable to sit still anymore, she got up and walked around, still trying to choke down the awful tea. She wandered into the living room and stopped in front of the fireplace. Lira never used to put up photographs, but since Amy had moved in, she had framed several pictures and lined them up on the mantle. They were pictures of Lira and Amy, mostly, but there were some with other Sadlers as well. There was a picture Luis had taken the day he helped Amy move out of her apartment, where they were standing on the sidewalk and Amy had grabbed Lira from behind and lifted her off her feet and they were both laughing. There was a picture of Amy's whole family at her nephew's third birthday party, Lira smiling at Amy's side. There was a shot Becky had taken of Amy and Lira hugging while Lira kissed Amy's cheek. There was even a picture Lira had trustingly asked a stranger to take when they were out on a date. They were standing in front of a restaurant, both wearing nice dresses, and Amy was behind Lira with her arms around her waist. Lira had her hands on Amy's, Amy had her face against Lira's hair, and they were both smiling happily, even though Amy had been terrified that the stranger would steal Lira's phone.

Amy turned away from the pictures and looked at her partner with tears streaming down her face.

"This is what she was proudest of," she said, her voice barely more than a whisper. "Us. The life we were making together. Her becoming part of my family. Us, me and her, together. She was so happy, Luis. We both were."

"Don't say 'was,' Amy. We'll get her back and you'll both be happy again."

"But he's *hurting* her." She forgot about the teacup she was holding and barely noticed when it fell from her hands, shattering on the floor. "I failed her, Luis. I should have seen this coming. I knew she was his type, but I still didn't think—"

"You didn't fail her. None of us are gonna fail her, okay?" He took Amy's arm, gently. "Forget about the cup for now. Let's go find Wheeler, see if any neighbors saw anything."

Amy nodded, gratefully following him to the door. She couldn't just sit here and cry. She had to take action, look for a lead. There had to be *something*.

"We'll get her back," Luis murmured as they walked, his hand on her back. "We'll find her. She'll be okay."

Amy tried hard to believe him, but she couldn't stop thinking about her sweet, beautiful Lira in the hands of the psychopath who had already tortured and killed three women, about their fruitless search that had already lasted six months. She didn't see how anything would ever be okay again.

***

That night, Amy found herself slumped at her desk, staring again at the picture of Lira taped to her monitor. The last time she had been here, just hours ago, all she could think about was the amazing sex she'd had with Lira the night before. She found herself going over it again in her mind, wondering how they had gone from pure bliss to absolute terror in such a short period of time. She wished she could rewind to last night and just pause there, with Lira safely in her arms forever.

As with the other missing women, the neighbors had been of no help. Most of them were at work when Lira was taken, and the few who had been home had been too absorbed in their own lives to notice anything unusual. Who wouldn't be?

Amy was still hoping for the best-case scenario: that they would find Lira before the bastard had the chance to do anything to her. Lira would be frightened, and there would be lingering effects from the trauma, but it was nothing they couldn't handle. She knew every hour that passed made that scenario less likely, however, and she couldn't stop thinking about the worst-case scenario: finding Lira's ravaged body behind a dumpster a few months from now.

They couldn't let that happen. They *couldn't*. But how were they supposed to stop it with so little to go on?

She jumped when her phone started buzzing on the desk. Maybe someone had found a lead? She answered the phone without even looking to see who it was.

"Amy?" said a woman's voice. "It's Genevieve, Lira's mom. Someone called me from the Brookwood Police Department to notify me that my daughter is missing. Is that true?"

Amy let out her breath. "Yeah. She's…she's missing."

"Do you have any idea what happened?"

"Yeah, we have some idea. I can't go into too much detail, but it's related to a case we've been working on for a while."

"Someone took her?"

"Yes. We're doing everything we can…I know it's not enough, but we're trying our best to bring her home."

"Is it…personal? Was it someone she knows?"

"No. No, it's someone who goes after strangers. It's not personal."

There was a pause. "Do you think she's alive?"

"Yeah, I'm pretty sure she's still alive. And I'm going to do everything I can to keep her that way."

"Do they want money? I can get you money. Whatever you need."

"No, this guy's not after money."

"He just wants her?"

"Yes."

Amy could hear Genevieve crying. "This is exactly the sort of thing I wanted to protect her from."

"What do you mean, protect her? Has anyone threatened her in the past?"

"No, no, I just mean as a mother, you want to protect your child from any kind of predator." She paused. "What should I do? Should I come out there?"

"No." Amy's voice hardened, against her will. "The time to do that would have been any of the times she asked you to come visit her. You could have spent time with her then. The only thing you'd do now is get in the way of the investigation."

There was silence for a moment. "You're right. I haven't been the best mother. Is there anything I *can* do?"

"Just wait. I'm going to find her even if it kills me, and maybe she'll want you then. Or maybe she won't. Just wait, and respect whatever she decides. That's all you can do."

"Okay," Genevieve said, sobbing. "Okay. I can do that."

Amy hung up the phone and looked up to see her own mother approaching. "Mom. How did you get in here?"

"I'm your mother," said Becky sternly, as if that explained it. "I brought you a sandwich."

"Thanks, Mom, but I don't really have an appetite."

"You know Lira wouldn't want you starving to death on her account."

"I know." Amy touched Lira's picture gently, tracing her face with her finger. "What if I never get to touch her again?"

"You can't think like that."

"But what if I don't? He's killed three women so far and we don't even know who he is, or where he is."

"You're a good detective. You'll find him."

"I need you to go by our house and feed Henry and Clea tonight, and maybe tomorrow too. And let Henry out in the yard at least."

"Okay. How much food do I give the cat?"

"Um, she usually measures it out, but it's okay if you just fill up the dish. And try not to act too stressed out. She says Clea won't eat in a stressful environment, and we need that cat to be in good health when Lira gets back." Her voice broke up a little on those last words.

"I'll try, but I *am* stressed."

Amy nodded sympathetically. "You know, I always used to hear people saying they loved someone more than life itself, and I didn't really get what they meant by that." She looked up at her mother. "I think I get it now."

"Oh, Amy." Becky pulled her daughter into her arms, and Amy started crying in earnest.

"She has to be so scared, Mom. And I can't help her."

"You need to let me take you home, Amy. You need to get some sleep."

"No." Amy pulled away. "I can sleep when Lira's back. Tonight I'm staying here and going over everything we have until I find something useful."

"You can't go without sleep forever."

Amy raised her eyebrows. "Then we better make sure Lira's not gone forever."

Chapter 14

Amy made sure she was in the lobby when the mail came the next day. She knew what was coming, and although she dreaded seeing it, it was the only way to find out anything about Lira. Luis insisted on coming with her. He was thinking more practically than she was and had brought an evidence bag and gloves. He kept glancing nervously at Amy like he thought she was going to go off the deep end any minute. Amy couldn't really blame him for that. She thought she might, too.

When the expected envelope arrived, however, it wasn't addressed to the Brookwood Police Department like the others. This one was addressed to Det. Amy Sadler.

"So he knows I'm Lira's girlfriend," she said dully.

"She might have told him."

"Why would she tell him that?"

"She might tell him anything under the influence of the ketamine." Luis carefully opened the envelope and slid out the picture.

It was Lira, all right. She was in the same bed the other three women had been photographed in, but she was flinching away from the camera.

"She didn't cooperate when he took her picture," Luis observed.

"That's my girl," said Amy softly. "Okay, flip it over."

"You sure?"

She was trembling violently, but she didn't see how she was going to get any readier. "I'm sure."

Please don't have any marks on the back, she thought. *Please, please, be the first one with no marks.*

Luis flipped the picture over.

There were two red tally marks on the back. Each one felt like a knife in Amy's chest. She turned around, ran into the bathroom, and threw up.

Amy wasn't sure how long she had been locked in the stall when her mother came looking for her. She knew she wasn't a pretty sight. She was curled up on the floor by the toilet, sobbing. It had actually crossed her mind that Lira would freak out if she saw her on the floor in such a germy place, but she felt like she deserved it. Lira had been raped, at least twice, probably more than that by now. She could only imagine the agony her sweet girlfriend was going through, and she had no way to stop it. It was supposed to be her job to protect Lira from things like this.

"Amy, Luis told me about the picture," Becky called through the door. "Can you please let me in?"

Amy reached up and unlocked the door. Her mother, apparently not interested in getting germy with her, pulled her to her feet before hugging her.

"He told me about the tally marks," Becky continued. "But it sounds like you don't know for sure what they really mean. Maybe they don't mean what you think they mean."

"Maybe," said Amy, but she didn't really believe it. She was just too tired to argue.

"At least you know she's alive."

"She just needs to stay that way long enough for me to find her." She shuddered, thinking of the victim who had died from a ketamine overdose. What if that happened to Lira? What if he gave her just a little too much and she stopped breathing and died in that awful place?

"She's a very strong woman." Becky stepped back and assessed her daughter's appearance. "You know you look like hell. Please let me take you home so you can rest, or at least let me get you something to eat."

"Not right now. I just want to be alone for a little bit."

She couldn't really be alone at her own desk, so she went to the morgue, taking Lira's keys with her so she could let herself into Lira's office. She wasn't prepared for the wave of emotion that swept over her as she entered the quiet room. Lira's desk looked like she'd just gotten up from it, like she'd be back any minute. There was a file folder sitting out, and her computer was still on, waiting for her to get back from lunch. *She'd still be here if I hadn't taken so long interviewing those witnesses*, Amy couldn't help thinking.

On Lira's desk were three framed pictures that she always said cheered her up: one of Clea, one of Amy in her uniform at some police event, and one of Lira and Amy smiling with their arms around each other. Amy picked up the last picture and collapsed onto the couch, wondering if Lira would ever smile like that again.

Amy knew she had to adjust her best-case scenario. Now the best scenario would be finding Lira right away, before she had to suffer too much more abuse. Amy knew they were going to have a very long road ahead of them even then. She'd been through her own share of traumatic experiences, not the least of them being when Daryl Flynn had attacked her. If the others hadn't finally remembered to do their damn jobs, Flynn would certainly have raped her and possibly even killed her, and she well remembered the terrifying moments when she believed that was exactly what would happen. It had taken her a long time to move past that, and sometimes she wasn't sure she really had. She would go entire days without thinking much about it. She had a scar on her wrist from where she'd strained too hard against the ropes that bound her and had cut herself deeply, and often she would glance at the scar and not even think about how she'd gotten it. But then some days, inexplicably, something would bring it up in her mind and she would suddenly feel the panic come rushing back in. Just like that, she would be full of shame and pain and fear again, and it could be very difficult to shake once it came back up. She wasn't sure it would ever really be over.

And now Lira, sweet, gentle Lira, was going to have the same kind of burden for the rest of her life. Amy hoped she had what it took to get her through it.

When she went back upstairs, she was filled with resolve. She noticed they had added a copy of Lira's picture to the display board, but she didn't linger there. She walked straight up to Luis.

"We're *going* to catch this son of a bitch," she told him. "We're going to get Lira out of there. And when we do, I am going to kill him. If he's unarmed when we catch him and he's cornered and he's not threatening us in any way, I'm still going to kill him. If you take my gun away, I will find something to stab him with. You cannot stop me. Am I clear?"

"Loud and clear," said Luis. "But, just between you and me, I'm not going to stand in your way."

Chapter 15

Amy couldn't remember quite when Lira had become the most important person in her life. She wasn't sure exactly when Lira had gone from being just someone she worked with, to a friend, to her best friend. She didn't know exactly when she had fallen in love with her, or when Lira had become someone she couldn't live without. But she knew when the letter came that she was going to do exactly what it said.

It came the day after the picture had arrived. Amy had spent two sleepless nights without Lira. She remembered Lira telling her once about the horrible things that happened to people who didn't sleep, something about hallucinations and eventual death, but it all seemed pretty minor compared to the ramifications of being without Lira. The letter, like the picture the day before, was addressed to Amy. It read:

Det. Amy Sadler –

She keeps calling your name. If you would like to see her again, I would be happy to reunite the two of you. It can happen only if you follow my instructions to the letter:

> *1. Meet me at Riverside Park tonight at 11 pm. Wait near the water. I will come only when I see you.*
> *2. You will come alone. If I see anyone else in the park, I will leave, and you will not see her again.*
> *3. You will come unarmed and without a cell phone or wire. I will search you.*
> *4. You will not be able to find her without me. Don't try anything stupid.*
> *5. You will come with me to my vehicle. If anyone follows us, I will kill you.*

"I have to do it," said Amy immediately. The others were silent, no doubt trying to think of a way to use the unsub's plan against him.

"I don't like it," said Wheeler. "It sounds like a trap. Why would he want you? You're not his type."

"He wouldn't want me on my own, but I'm sure all sorts of pervy ideas popped into his head when he found out Lira was in a lesbian relationship."

"It's too dangerous. We can't let you do it, Amy. If we try to monitor you, he may find out and kill you. If we don't, he'll take you away and we may never see you again."

Amy shrugged. "I'm willing to take that risk. At least I'd be with Lira."

"We can't send you away, unarmed, with no idea where he's taking you."

"If we don't do it the way he says, we might lose our only chance of finding Lira alive," insisted Amy. "Look, I'm pretty good at getting myself out of situations. I mean, I've been a cop for a decade now. I've gotten into all kinds of trouble, but I've always managed to get back out." Wheeler met her eyes, and she knew he was thinking of the time when she couldn't possibly have gotten away on her own. She held his gaze. "I can't just leave her there alone," she said quietly.

Luis had been silent the whole time, doing something on his computer. Now he rejoined the others. "I think I know a way we can track her and still follow the directions," he said. "I know someone who can lend us a pocket-sized GPS tracker. If you put it in your shoe, he probably won't find it when he searches you, but we'll be able to see exactly where you are on our computer. So you can actually meet him on your own, and we can give you guys a head start, but then we can follow and get you and Lira out."

Amy stepped forwards and threw her arms around Luis. "Thank you," she said in his ear.

She felt anxious on the way to the river that night, but she found she wasn't really scared of what might happen to her. She felt pure hatred towards the man she was going to meet; there wasn't any room left to be frightened of him. Her only fear was of something going wrong with the rescue operation.

They had prepared as much as they could. Luis got the GPS tracker and set up the app that would allow him to track her location online. Amy had put the tracker in her sock and walked around the neighborhood for a bit to make sure they could track her successfully. The others promised not to tell her mother what she was doing if she showed up to check on Amy again, and Luis volunteered to drive her to a point a half mile from the park. She left her phone and gun with him before getting out to walk the rest of the way.

"Listen," he said, "I know the last time you did something like this, it didn't go very well, but I want you to know that I'm a better partner than Mitch. I've got your back."

"You'd better. It's not just my life on the line this time. It's Lira's." She smiled tiredly. "But I know you're better than Mitch. I'll see you soon," she promised him.

"You'd better," he said. "Otherwise your mom will kill me for letting you do this. She's even scarier than you when she's mad."

"Don't worry. The bastard's clearly getting overconfident. I mean, we're going to be two against one. He doesn't stand a chance."

"But Lira's being drugged, and he'll try to drug you too."

"And I know it's coming, so I'm ready for him. *And* I have backup. You know how you said he'd make a mistake eventually?"

Luis nodded.

"Well, this is his mistake." Amy hugged her partner and took off without looking back.

Riverside Park wasn't too big; just a grassy area next to the river that had a few picnic tables and a modest playground. There were few trees, so you could clearly see the entire park from the parking area, and vice versa. She couldn't see her watch in the dark, so she didn't really know how long she spent pacing around by the water before she finally saw the dark figure coming towards her. She froze and waited, resisting the urge to tackle him and strangle him the way he'd strangled his victims. She had to keep her anger under control until she knew where Lira was.

"Detective Sadler, I presume?" he said as he got closer. She noticed that he was pointing a gun at her, but she didn't mind. It just gave her a weapon to potentially turn on him later.

"That's me. I assume you heard about me from Lira?"

"She does seem to miss you quite a bit. I remember your name from the newspaper, though. You're one of the detectives investigating my case. I trust you've been enjoying my pictures?" He was big, blond, obnoxiously sure of himself. His hands were huge and rough. Lira would not have stood a chance against him. Nevertheless, Amy thought she saw a scratch across his face.

"It's nice to be kept up to date." Amy stood still while he patted her down. She was careful not to react, even when he lingered too long in unpleasant places. She didn't even complain when he tied her hands behind her before walking her to his car. He took a lot of unnecessary turns as he drove, no doubt trying to make sure they weren't being followed. Amy hoped her tracking device was still working.

"She's sleeping at the moment," he said conversationally. "But I'm sure she'll be pleased to see you when she wakes up."

"Her name is Lira. Why won't you say her name?" He didn't answer. "Is this how you are with all of them? Does not saying their names make it easier to kill them?"

"If names are so important to you, why haven't you asked for mine?"

"I don't actually give a fuck what your name is."

"See? You understand."

Amy was quiet for a minute. She supposed she did understand. Before she was dying to know his name, but now, what did it matter? She was just going to kill him anyway.

"So what made you want me?" she asked him. "That's not your MO."

"I decided it was time to branch out." He drove out of the city limits into the farmland beyond

"One woman's not enough for you anymore?"

"It's enough, but I was presented with a new opportunity." His lips curled into a smile.

"To have a lesbian couple."

He nodded. "I didn't know she was a lesbian when I took her, but she kept yelling for 'Amy' when she got scared, especially when she first woke up. I never had someone call a woman's name before, so I asked her who Amy was. She said it's her girlfriend, who loves her and would never let anyone hurt her." He smiled again, his tone mocking. "I knew if you loved her that much, you'd come."

"What do you think we're going to do, fuck each other while you watch?"

He chuckled. "You won't have much choice. It's always interested me, you know. The relationship between two women."

"You really think you can keep two women in line? You're going to be outnumbered now."

His jaw clenched. "I could keep more than that in line."

"Even if one's a cop?"

He glanced at her and laughed. "Without your gun, you're just a regular girl."

He turned off the county road and parked behind an old, dilapidated house, ushering Amy inside with the gun to her back. Once indoors, he untied her hands. "You go first," he told her. "Up the stairs, to the room at the end of the hall."

Amy walked slowly up the stairs, hoping he would continue to believe he was controlling her with the gun and the promise of Lira for just a little longer. As soon as he decided to break out the ketamine, she was going to be as defenseless as all his other victims. But she *could not* go on the attack until she had confirmed that Lira was there.

She froze at the top of the stairs. There was a light on in the room at the end of the hall, and she could see Lira lying motionless on the same iron bed they'd seen in the pictures. She couldn't tell from where she stood if Lira was alive or dead, but her next move had to be the same regardless.

In one smooth motion, she spun around and punched her captor between the eyes, knocking him down the stairs. She ran down after him and grabbed his gun as it fell.

"No, please!" he said, holding his hands up as she raised the gun.

"'Please?'" repeated Amy, her voice shaking. "I bet that's

what Lira said to you, isn't it?"

He looked at her, but didn't say anything.

"*ANSWER ME!* Did she plead with you to stop hurting her?" Her voice broke.

"Y-yes," he admitted.

"And did you stop?"

"No, I—"

"That's what I thought." She took the safety off, feeling like a woman possessed. "Say it again."

"Please," he said uncertainly. "Don't shoot. I'll—"

Without waiting for him to finish, she fired the gun at his crotch, destroying the body part he had used as a weapon on at least four women. He screamed shrilly, his hands flying down to the wound, face contorted in agony and horror. Unmoved, Amy raised the gun again and shot him through the heart, shot him three times just to make sure. Then she turned on her heel and ran upstairs as fast as she could, down the hall to the room with the iron bed.

Lira still wasn't moving, even after the gunshots. For one horrible moment Amy thought she had arrived too late, but then she felt Lira's pulse. She was alive; just heavily drugged.

Amy gently pulled the blanket back to assess Lira's injuries. A part of her had still been hoping that he hadn't actually touched her, but that hope was quickly dashed. She was completely naked, with angry bruises on her shoulders and arms, bite marks on her breasts, and six ugly tally marks cut into her skin, just above her heart. The last one was still bleeding. The skin around them was red and swollen, and Amy noticed it was hot to the touch when she instinctively reached out to wipe the blood away, wanting to make her better somehow. One of her own tears splashed onto Lira's chest. It made her think of fairy tales she'd heard as a child where the tears of one person magically healed the wounds of another, and she fervently, absurdly, wished it could be true in real life. She wanted to make it all go away, to make Lira whole and happy like she was the last time she saw her. She wanted to kiss her and make her wake up.

She pulled the blanket back further and felt her heart break even more as she saw the rest of the evidence of the torture her sweet girlfriend had been through. There were bruises and blood marking her tender inner thighs, her right knee looked swollen, and her right ankle was cuffed to the bedframe, purple bruises on her skin to show how she had strained against it. Amy noticed then that Lira's right wrist was badly swollen and discolored, and for some reason, this enraged her more than anything else. *He broke her damn wrist*, she thought. *How could he possibly have needed to break her wrist?* She was tempted to go back downstairs and shoot him again, even though he had to be dead already, but her desire to stay by Lira's side won out. She gently covered Lira back up with the blanket and sat beside her, stroking her hair, until she heard the others arriving.

Luis's relief was palpable when he saw his partner coming down the stairs, but Amy went past him to Wheeler. "I need your coat," she told him.

"My coat?" He began taking it off despite his confusion.

"I need it for her. She's alive, but…"

"Take it then." He pushed it into her hands and she ran upstairs to put it on Lira. She didn't want to move Lira's broken wrist any more than necessary, so she just put her left arm in the sleeve and buttoned up the coat. It looked huge on her, but that was good; it meant she was covered. It meant that, no matter how humiliating the experience might be for her, at least her coworkers wouldn't see her naked.

"Is it okay to come in?" Luis called from the hallway.

"Yeah, I guess so."

He stepped through the doorway, saw Lira in Wheeler's coat, and averted his eyes. "I'm sorry, Amy."

"She's alive. That's the most important thing. I was so scared I would never see her alive again."

"You did a good job. We thought we were coming to rescue you, but you had it under control. And you killed him, just like you said you would."

"Yes, but not slowly enough." She tried to smile at him, but found she couldn't yet. "If you didn't have that tracking device, I might not have been able to do this. I'm going to tell her that, that you saved her just as much as I did."

"You can tell her, but you know she's going to see you as the hero anyway."

"I hope she can still see me as a hero after I let her get hurt like this." She pulled the edge of the blanket away, revealing Lira's cuffed ankle. "Could you…"

"Yeah, I got it." Luis walked around the bed, pulling out his keys, and easily unlocked the handcuffs holding Lira to the bed.

Amy breathed a sigh of relief. "Thanks."

"No problem." They heard sirens approaching. "That'll be the ambulance," said Luis. He put a hand on Amy's shoulder. "I know it doesn't look like it right now, but she's going to be okay. She has you."

Amy nodded, but she didn't know if it was true.

After Luis went back downstairs, the EMTs came up. Amy tried to stay out of the way as they took Lira's vital signs and strapped her onto the gurney, answering their questions as calmly as she could. She followed them when they carried her downstairs, past the dead body of her attacker, through the door to the waiting ambulance. Amy paused in the doorway, watching Lira's face lit up by the flashing red and blue lights as her head lolled helplessly to the side. Suddenly she turned around and ran back in the house, straight to the body of the man who had done this to the woman she loved, and started kicking him fiercely.

"Amy, Amy, stop!" She felt someone grab her from behind and realized it was Wheeler. "Amy, stop kicking him! He's dead! There's nothing else you can do!"

She struggled to get away from him, but he wouldn't let go. Finally, at a loss for words, she simply motioned to the door and whispered, "My Lira."

"I know," Wheeler said softly. "But there's nothing else you can do to him. She needs you right now. Go to her."

She nodded and pulled away, choking back a sob as she went out to the ambulance.

***

The quiet hospital room was a relief after the fast-paced emergency room. The tox screen had shown high levels of benzodiazepines in Lira's system, which was why she was still out, but they thought she'd come to before long. Amy couldn't wait to see those beautiful eyes open, to talk to her girlfriend again, but she was also scared. She didn't know how Lira would be doing emotionally, and she couldn't stop thinking about what the letter said. *She keeps calling your name.* Sweet Lira, in her drugged and confused state, must have been wondering where Amy was, why she wasn't coming to save her. She wasn't sure she deserved Lira anymore, but if Lira still wanted her, of course she would stay. She hoped Lira would let her stay forever. Amy could see now that she had wasted too much time. She'd been enjoying their relationship as it was, afraid to ask for more when she already had so much, but she realized now that it wasn't just about asking more for herself. It was also about giving more to Lira, and Lira deserved to know that Amy planned to be by her side for the rest of her life. For the first time, Amy let herself think, just for a moment, about the possibility of marrying Lira.

But a moment was all she had. There was too much to worry about in the present. Lira would be here in the hospital for at least a few days. She looked relatively peaceful right now, lying in bed with the IV in her hand, which was giving her antibiotics to quell the nasty infection from the cuts and to prevent her from developing the most common STDs (the previous victims had tested negative for STDs in autopsy, so he probably had none to give her, but it was better to be safe than sorry). She had a cast on her wrist now (a spiral fracture. He had twisted her wrist, had broken it intentionally), and they had stitched up the worst vaginal tear. When she woke up, they would offer her emergency contraception and pain medication. Later there would be follow-up visits and more tests. She would have to consider counseling, antidepressants. This was only the beginning.

In a way, Amy was glad Lira had slept through everything so far. Even the medical staff had agreed that it was better for her to be sedated, especially for the rape kit. Amy had been terrified that she would wake up in the middle of it all and be frightened, but fortunately that hadn't happened.

She took Lira's hand – carefully, not wanting to disturb the IV port – and kissed her fingers. With her other hand she gently stroked Lira's hair, trailing her fingers down a soft cheek. This was how Lira was meant to be touched: gently, lovingly. Never, ever any other way.

The pain of seeing her love like this felt physical to Amy. It started in her heart and went all the way down to the tips of her fingers.

"My sweet girl," she whispered. "I love you so, so much."

And then, finally, Lira began to stir.

Chapter 16

When Lira woke up and saw Amy, she didn't know at first if she was real or not. She'd had a few hallucinations under the influence of the ketamine, and most of them involved Amy. She reached out to touch Amy with her left hand, to see if she was real. She had to use her left hand even though something was stuck to the back of it because her right hand still didn't work. It didn't hurt so much right now, but it was heavy. She touched Amy's face and it felt real, solid. It felt like Amy's face.

Amy took Lira's hand and held it against her skin. She looked down at Lira and her eyes were sad, or happy. Happy and sad. She said, "Hey! Welcome back."

Lira worked to move her tongue. It felt thicker than it should. "Amy," she said slowly. "What happened?"

"We came and got you," said Amy. "You're safe now. We're at the hospital."

She looked around the sterile room and then down at herself, noticing the cast on her right wrist and the IV port in her left hand. Then she looked back at Amy. "I knew," she said, her words coming out slurred. "I knew you would come." She struggled to push herself into a sitting position.

"Lira, be careful," fussed Amy. "You have two cracked ribs."

"I don't care. I missed you." Lira let herself fall forwards, throwing her arms awkwardly around Amy. Amy wrapped her in a fast hug, and Lira finally, *finally*, felt safe.

She let herself stay there for a long time without talking, but then her head started to clear a little, and she had questions she needed answered.

"How long?" she asked, her voice a little stronger now. "How long was I there?"

"Three days and two nights. Too long, but not nearly as long as the women before you."

"How did you...find me?"

"He sent a letter saying he wanted to 'reunite' us, that you were asking for me. So I met him and let him take me to you. Luis gave me a tracking chip so they could follow me."

"Did you arrest him?"

"Better. I killed him."

Lira numbly thought over what memories she had from the last few days. She tugged at her hospital gown and noticed her tally marks had been covered with a bandage.

"He cut me," said Lira uncertainly.

"I know, baby. I saw."

"How many were there?"

"Six," said Amy, cringing a little.

Six. He had raped her six times. That felt like a lot, but it was a lot less than 314 times. "I don't remember getting the marks," she told Amy. "I would just wake up and there would be a new one."

"Good. It's better that you don't remember."

"Maybe, but I was so frustrated. I couldn't make it stop. I tried to find a way out, but my ankle was chained to the bed, and the bed was bolted down, and I couldn't get away." She felt panic rising in her, the same panic she had felt in that terrible house.

"It's okay, sweetie," Amy promised, rubbing Lira's back. "I know you did everything you could. There was no way for you to get out of there by yourself."

"You know…you know what he did to me?"

Amy nodded, blinking back tears. "I know."

"But you still want to be with me?"

Amy frowned. "Why wouldn't I?"

"I'm *broken*."

"So? I've felt broken before. It's not forever."

"I know it's not logical, but I feel…ruined."

Amy looked at her for a moment. "Scoot over," she said. "I'm joining you."

Lira carefully scooted over to one side of the bed, the same side she would have been on if they were at home in their real bed. Amy stretched out beside her, carefully working her way around the IV tube.

"I can't sleep without you next to me anymore, did you know that?" said Amy. "I haven't slept a wink since you've been gone."

"I slept, but only because he was drugging me."

"It'll be good for us both to get some normal sleep," said Amy. She kissed Lira's face gently. "I love you," she said softly, taking Lira's hand in hers. "I love everything about you." She kissed Lira's hand. "I love you more than anything." She carefully laced her fingers through Lira's. "And you will never, *ever* be ruined to me."

OUT OF THE SHADOWS

Chapter 17

Amy was still wide awake when her mother arrived the next morning, but thankfully, Lira had finally gone to sleep. Becky found Amy lying on the bed with her arms protectively around Lira, whose head was resting on Amy's chest. Amy waved to acknowledge her mother's arrival and then put a finger to her lips. Becky tiptoed to the side of the bed and set down the bouquet of flowers and the bag she had brought with her.

"I brought the things you asked for from home," she whispered.

"Thanks," Amy whispered back. She glanced down at Lira. "I've never had to pee so bad in my life."

"So go pee!"

"I can't! She just fell asleep an hour ago!"

"Fine, pee the bed then." Becky sat down.

Amy continued lying in silence for a bit, hating to admit that her mother was right, before finally giving up.

"Okay, help me move her," she whispered. "But *be careful*."

"Do you think I don't know that?" Becky moved around the bed and helped Amy slowly ease Lira onto her back. "She's out cold, poor thing."

"She should be, after the night we had," Amy muttered, hurrying towards the bathroom. When she came back out, Becky grabbed her arm and dragged her out into the hall.

"How is she doing?" the older woman asked.

"She's...bad, but not really any worse than you would expect." Amy pushed her hair out of her face. "She's in a lot of pain. They gave her pain meds, but all they really do is take the edge off. And she's really anxious. It took her hours to fall asleep. Every time she started to drift off, she would kind of jump back awake in combat mode, like she thought someone was attacking her. She didn't go to sleep for real until after they brought breakfast. Which she didn't touch." She looked down. "And I figured out pretty fast that I can't touch her when she's not expecting it."

Becky took her daughter's hands. "Amy, I'm sorry this

happened to you both. But she *will* get better."

"I wish I could bring the sick bastard back to life."

"Why would you want to do that?"

"So I can break his wrist and then kill him again. I'm sure you noticed the cast on Lira's wrist?"

Becky nodded.

"It's a spiral fracture. That means he twisted her wrist until it broke. Thanks to the drugs he gave her, she doesn't remember very much of what he did to her, but she *does* remember that. And I just shot him straight through the heart. He didn't suffer. He died right away."

"Amy, you're a good person. I know you don't really want to make people suffer."

Amy shook her head. "We all have a dark side, Mom. Well, everyone except Lira. And when people hurt Lira, it brings out my dark side. I did what I had to do at the time, but I wish, I really wish, I could have made him suffer for what he did to her. Because *she* has to, and she didn't do anything wrong." Her voice broke and she stopped talking.

Becky squeezed Amy's hands. "Why don't you let me sit with Lira for a while, and you go take a walk outside. It might help you to clear your head."

Amy glanced into the room. Lira had curled into a ball, but she appeared to still be sleeping. "It might be nice to move around a little," she admitted. "But I'm going to stay on the property, okay? If she asks for me, just give me a call and I'll be right back up here."

"I will."

"And if she wakes up while I'm gone, see if you can get her to eat something."

So Amy reluctantly tore herself away from the hospital room that held the love of her life. Perhaps it *would* be nice to get a little break while Lira was sleeping. It had been a stressful night. Lira had been a little disoriented when she first woke up, but as the drugs wore off and she became more alert, she also became more frightened. She kept looking towards the door as if expecting her attacker to come in and reclaim her, although Amy assured her repeatedly that the man was dead and couldn't hurt her anymore. She was also in intense pain. She asked her nurse for an ice pack, which Amy thought at first was for her banged-up knee, but instead she had placed it between her legs. Amy didn't like to think about how much pain a person would have to be in to want to put ice *there*. Lira had also cried off and on, as if the reality of the situation kept hitting her and breaking her heart every time. But at least she was turning to Amy for comfort, rather than withdrawing as some might have done. And she didn't seem to blame Amy at all for letting this happen to her.

Amy walked around outside for a little bit, but all she really wanted to do was go back upstairs and be with Lira. As outraged as she was that any of this had happened, she was also overwhelmed with gratitude that she had gotten Lira back alive and that it hadn't taken weeks or months. So she went back inside, stopping briefly at the gift shop to buy a box of markers. On her way upstairs, she ran into Wheeler at the elevator.

"I was just coming up to find you," he said. "How is Lira?"

"She has the same injuries as the others, plus a couple cracked ribs and a broken wrist. And she's scared to death, but who wouldn't be?"

"Sounds like she fought back harder than the others."

"Of course she did. She'd already seen the end result, three times. So what did you find in the house?"

"Well, we identified the unsub as Jared Nielson. We also found his supply of ketamine and a cache of Ativan. We're not sure about the Ativan, but the ketamine came from a veterinary clinic. Shouldn't be too hard for Narcotics to pin down who was stealing it."

Amy stiffened. "Whoever supplied him with the drugs is partly responsible for what happened to Lira."

"I know, and I know you want to go all *Man on Fire* on everyone who played any kind of role in this, but you know we can't let you do that. Narcotics will take care of it, and you're not even on the case anymore." Amy started to protest, but Wheeler held up his hands. "You know you can't stay on this case, Amy. Not when your significant other is one of the victims. It was one thing when we were looking for her, but now we found her, and I'm placing you on leave. Your job is to be with her right now. I'll keep you in the loop as long as I know you're not going to do anything crazy."

"*Okay*," Amy grumbled in frustration. "Did you find anything else?"

"We found the obligatory scrapbook. It had newspaper articles, and pictures he didn't send us."

"Please tell me there weren't any of Lira."

"There…may have been a couple."

"Wheeler, you have to get rid of them before anyone else sees them. We don't really need them for evidence. The perp's dead. There won't be a trial."

She could tell from the look on Wheeler's face that he was about to tell her something she wouldn't like. "You know we can't do that. And anyway, there may be a component to the case that we haven't actually solved yet."

She narrowed her eyes. "What do you mean?"

"We think he may have been communicating with someone else."

"He didn't have a partner, did he?" She started to pace. "We only found DNA from one guy on all of our victims. It *was* the guy I killed, wasn't it?"

"We're double checking that, but we don't think he was actually working with someone else. It's more like he was *competing* with someone else. Some of the articles he had were for unsolved murders around Chicago that overlap with his kills, but the MO is different. The tally marks Nielson left on his victims may not have just been for his own sick pleasure. That may have been him bragging to the other guy."

"So, was this a friendly competition? Is this guy going to come to Brookwood now and try to finish the job with Lira, or, or bump me off because I whacked his buddy?"

"We don't know yet. As soon as I know something, I'll tell you. In the meantime, I'll post a uniform outside Lira's room, just to be safe."

"Thank you. But could you tell them to maybe try and stay out of her sight? I don't want her to know she could still be in danger."

"I'll see what I can do."

She managed a tired smile. "I'd better get back upstairs." She held up her new markers. "I'm going to decorate Lira's cast for her, so when she looks at it she can think of something other than what it felt like to have her wrist broken."

"I didn't know you had any artistic talent."

"I don't, so…it should be interesting." She got into the elevator and punched the button for Lira's floor. On the way up she considered the situation. It was a serious blow to hear that someone else might be after Lira, but it just meant Amy had to be a lot smarter than she'd been before. Under no circumstances should Lira be anywhere on her own until this man was caught. But she would certainly be off work for a while, until she had recovered enough, physically and emotionally, to do her usual duties. And Amy was on leave now, so she should be able to stay by Lira's side 24/7. All she had to do was make sure her weapon was always within reach, and there would be no way in hell anyone was going to touch Lira. Hopefully they would bring him down quickly enough to keep Lira from ever having to know about him.

Suddenly her blood froze. Lira was alone right now. Well, Amy's mom was with her, but what was *she* going to do, knock the guy out with her purse? How *stupid* was Amy to think she could just go out for some fresh air and leave her girlfriend defenseless?

The second the elevator doors opened, Amy went barreling out, racing down the maze of hallways until she found the room that was Lira's. She slammed on the brakes just outside the doorway as she caught sight of her mother calmly leafing through a *People* magazine while Lira continued to sleep.

"You okay?" Becky asked her breathless daughter as she came into the room.

"Yeah," said Amy. "I'm fine." She gently pressed her lips to Lira's head and then got to work on her cast.

Chapter 18

This time when Lira woke up, her head felt much clearer, for better or worse. Amy was dozing in a chair next to the bed, and according to the clock on the wall, it was just past one in the afternoon. She noticed flowers on the nightstand and took the card out to see who they were from. She smiled slightly when she read the note from Becky, and then she noticed an even bigger note on her cast that could only be from Amy. There was a giant black *I*, followed by a big red heart, followed by the word *YOU*. She smiled again. There was always something satisfying about seeing Amy get sappy.

Amy stirred in her chair and opened her eyes. She saw Lira looking at her and smiled. "Hey," she said. "You slept through my mom's visit. Don't worry, though. She'll be back."

"I saw the flowers she brought. That was very sweet."

"She says she'll bring brownies next time." Amy looked at the clock. "Well, you didn't eat breakfast. Do you want lunch?"

Lira shook her head. "I'm not hungry."

"Well, I am." Amy picked up the hospital cafeteria menu. "How about I order, and you eat off my plate like you normally do?"

"Okay."

Amy called down to the cafeteria to order her lunch and then started going through a bag. "I had Mom bring us some stuff from home," she said. "She brought me a change of clothes. I guess I need to put them on at some point."

Lira looked at her. "You're still wearing what you had on the last time I saw you."

"Yeah, well, I haven't had time to worry about anything but finding you."

Lira remembered seeing Amy get dressed that morning, the day she was taken. She remembered them eating breakfast, and driving to work together. She remembered kissing Amy before they got out of the car, and getting the text from Amy later saying to have lunch without her. She remembered going home, and then leaving to go back to work, and being grabbed from behind while she locked the back door, the needle going in her arm.

"Lira!" Amy's voice broke through, and suddenly Lira was back in the hospital room, hyperventilating. "Lira, breathe," said Amy, grabbing her shoulders. "It's okay. You're safe. You're with me."

Lira struggled to slow down her breathing. She put her good hand on Amy's arm and felt her warmth until it drew her back to the present. Amy pulled her into a hug.

"I'm so sorry, Lira," murmured Amy, rubbing her back. "I'm sorry this happened. I wish I'd been there to protect you."

"It's not your fault." Lira clung to Amy, shaking. "You came and got me. That's all that matters."

"I wish I could have gotten you sooner, though." Amy kissed Lira's head and stroked her matted hair. "Mom brought your hairbrush. Do you want me to brush your hair for you?"

Lira nodded. Amy pulled the brush out of the bag and began carefully working the tangles out of Lira's long, auburn hair. Her gentle touch had a calming effect. Lira could see a profound sadness in Amy's eyes, but she still looked at Lira adoringly. It made her feel hopeful to see that Amy could still look at her that way after everything that had happened.

"There, much better," said Amy, putting the brush down. "Although it really needs to be washed. I bet you wouldn't mind taking a bath." Lira nodded. "Well, there is a tub in your bathroom. I can talk to the nurse, see if we can get something to go over your cast."

"Did they get all the…evidence?"

Amy gave her a pained look. "Yes, sweetie. They did all that when you first got here. You were unconscious, but I was there with you as much as they let me be. They did everything they were supposed to."

Lira nodded. "Okay. Just making sure."

The food came and Lira tried to eat, but all she managed was a French fry. Then Amy got the nurse to come unhook Lira's IV and put a plastic bag over her cast so she would be able to take a bath. Amy started running the water and came back to get Lira. "Well, there aren't any bath salts, and there isn't any organic volumizing shampoo from Fiji or whatever it is you use, but there's some really basic soap and some better-than-nothing shampoo in there."

Lira smiled. "I'm not in any position to complain, just as long as the water's hot."

Amy helped Lira to the bathroom, closing and locking the door behind them. She untied Lira's gown in the back, but when it started to slip away, Lira glimpsed the bruises and bite marks and hastily covered herself back up.

"Lira," said Amy softly, putting her hand on Lira's back. "It's okay. I already saw."

Lira turned to face her. She was shaking violently again. "I...I look really bad."

"Not to me." Amy touched her face. "When you really love someone, you see them as whole even when they're broken. You have to trust that that's how I see you right now."

Lira nodded uncertainly. She let Amy take the gown off and help her into the tub. The hot water was soothing, but she found the strength had gone out of her. She leaned helplessly against Amy.

"Hey, you're okay. You're okay," promised Amy. "I've got you." She held Lira, kissed her, stroked her hair until Lira felt strong enough to sit up on her own again.

"I was glad to see you were sleeping earlier," Lira remarked as Amy washed her hair. "You need to sleep. Maybe after this you can lie down on the bed, and I'll stay awake and let you sleep."

"You're the one in the hospital. Why don't you let me do the worrying?"

"But I can't help worrying. I love you too much."

"I really don't deserve you." Amy rinsed Lira's hair and carefully wiped off the smeared remnants of the makeup Lira had been wearing the day she was taken. "There's my beautiful girl!" she said when she was done. Lira smiled at her – not a real smile, of course; she hadn't smiled for real since her abduction – but enough to let Amy know she appreciated what she had said. She focused on Amy's touch and felt her shaking subside.

"I'm sorry I hit you last night," she said, breaking the stillness. While trying unsuccessfully to sleep, Lira had reverted several times to thinking she was still with her abductor. The first time, Amy had reached out to comfort her, with disastrous consequences.

"It's okay," said Amy. "You didn't know where you were, and you *should* hit people who are trying to hurt you. It made me kind of proud even if it did hurt a little."

"I gave you an epistaxis."

"A what?"

"A bloody nose."

"And it stopped bleeding, so everything's fine. Now I know to talk to you first before I try to touch you so you know it's me."

Lira sighed. "Does everyone at work know what happened to me?"

"Well, everyone who was working on the case knows, and maybe some other people too. Unfortunately, you became part of the case. Why do you ask?"

"I just...it's kind of humiliating. When I go back to work, people will see me and think of what happened."

"I think they'll see you and be glad you're back."

"You don't think they'll look at me differently?"

"Well, a serial killer took you, but you're still alive, so they might see you as being a little more badass than they originally thought."

Lira smiled a little in spite of herself. "I'm not badass."

"Yeah you are. You just hide it well." Amy helped Lira out of the water and toweled her off. "Look, they brought you a new gown," she said, holding it up. "It's *very* fashionable. Get ready to be the belle of the ball."

"It *will* be nice to wear real clothes again when I get out of here," Lira admitted, slipping into the gown and letting Amy tie it in the back. "I don't even know what happened to the dress I had on when..."

"It's okay. We'll get you a new one just like it." Amy helped Lira back into bed. "Do you think it'd be okay if I took a shower here? I really need one."

"Technically I don't think visitors are supposed to use the patient bathrooms, but I promise not to tell on you."

"I'll be quick."

Lira's nurse came in to hook her IV back up, but she didn't say anything about Amy being in the shower. When she left, Lira picked up the remote and started flipping channels, listening to the reassuring sound of the shower running. This was the sort of ordinary sound she was used to at home, the kind of sound that meant Amy was nearby and everything was as it should be. It seemed like a lifetime had passed since she'd last heard it.

"Amy," she said softly when her girlfriend emerged from the bathroom, toweling off her hair. "Does my mother know anything about what happened?"

"She knows you were kidnapped. Someone from the station notified her, and she called me to confirm it."

"But she doesn't know any details?"

"Not really. I told her I couldn't go into detail. Do you want me to call her?"

Lira shook her head. "I don't really want her to know details."

"Okay. Well, if you change your mind, let me know. I'll call whoever you want."

Lira nodded. "Was she…worried about me?"

"Yeah, of course! She asked if she should come out here."

"She wanted to come *here*?"

"Yeah. I told her to wait until we found you and see if you wanted her to come. She will, if you want her to."

Lira shook her head uncertainly. "She can't come now. I don't want her to see me like this."

"Well, I did kinda tell her that a better time would have been literally any of the times you asked."

"Why wouldn't she come before, but she wants to come now?"

Amy shrugged. "Sometimes people don't realize they're being assholes until something really awful happens."

"I suppose I *should* call her."

"When you're ready. Not sooner."

Lira nodded and pulled back the blankets. "Lie down with me. You need more sleep."

Amy got into bed and slid her arms around Lira. "What are we watching?"

"It's an Italian movie."

"Subtitles. That *will* put me to sleep!"

"Good. I promise not to hit you this time. I'll stay awake."

"You don't have to stay awake. I won't scare you again."

"But if I forget where I am again—"

"Don't worry. I've survived much worse." Amy kissed Lira's head. "I always say I love everything about you. That means I'm obligated to love the nosebleed you gave me."

Lira pondered that. "Do you also love it when I talk about nerdy stuff?"

"Of course. It's actually kinda cute when you go on about space and time machines and stuff."

"What about when I use scientific terms you don't understand?"

"It's like having my own personal Google, only *so* much sexier."

"Do you love that I'm such a stickler for following rules?"

"Are you kidding? You're the most moral person I've ever met. Everyone wants a girlfriend as trustworthy as you. *I'm* actually living the dream."

"What about when I correct your grammar? Do you love that?"

"How else will I learn?"

Lira giggled for the first time in days. It hurt her ribs, but she didn't care. She kissed Amy on the lips, another first since the abduction. "I love you," she whispered.

Amy stared into her eyes, and in that moment, she didn't look at Lira with sadness. Her eyes were full of love and

113

amazement, the look that Lira lived for. "I love you too," she said.

And for a just little while, in Lira's mind, there was no Italian movie on television, no hospital room, no IV stand by the bed or nurses walking by the door, not even any pain or fear. There wasn't anything in the world but Amy.

Chapter 19

Two days later, Lira was released from the hospital. Amy couldn't wait to get her back home so they could regain some sense of normalcy. Becky brought real clothes for Lira to change into, Amy brushed her hair neatly, and between the two of them, they had Lira looking almost ready for a night on the town by the time the nurse wheeled her downstairs.

When they got in the house, Lira looked around at all her familiar things as though she hardly recognized them. She wandered through the living room, dining room, and kitchen, then froze for a minute, staring at the back door. Amy was worried she was having another intense flashback, but she snapped out of it when she saw Clea running towards her. She immediately lit up and knelt down to talk to her.

"I wish she looked at me the way she looks at that cat," Amy muttered to Becky, but she was amused. She hadn't been in the house either since discovering that Lira was missing, and now she found herself looking around with gratitude. She had hoped not to come back here without Lira, and she didn't have to.

Over the next few days, they tried to pick up their lives where they had left off, but it wasn't easy. Lira slept little and ate even less. When she did sleep, it usually didn't take long for the nightmares to come. This was the worst part for Amy, because it gave her a glimpse of what Lira's ordeal must have been like for her. Lira would suddenly start screaming or crying, her hands raised to fend off an invisible attacker. Amy could only wake her by calling her name; to touch her in those moments was to become the attacker. Even if Lira was able to get back to sleep after that, Amy certainly couldn't. She would lie awake hating Jared Nielson, thinking, *she cried like that when he was hurting her, and he didn't even care.*

Amy was hopeful that there would be progress, though. Lira was signed up to see a therapist who specialized in working with survivors of sexual assault. She was going to go twice a week for now, and while she left her first session in a rather dark mood, the grounding techniques she gave her to work on really did seem to help her come back a little faster when she had a flashback. It was sometimes difficult for her to make it back without help, though, so Amy didn't dare leave her in the house alone. The first time Amy decided to go run errands, she waited for her mom to get off work and come over so Lira would still have someone nearby. Taking Lira with her didn't seem to be an option yet. She had asked, but Lira didn't want to go out in public. It was as if she thought the shame of her ordeal was written on her face and could be plainly read by anyone who looked at her. She didn't seem keen on having visitors either. Amy was worried she was becoming too withdrawn, but, as with the eating and sleeping problems, she didn't know what she could do about it.

She came home that evening to find her mother cooking dinner, Luis standing in the kitchen, and Lira nowhere in sight.

"Lira went upstairs to lie down," Becky said as soon as she saw her daughter.

She probably went upstairs not long after Luis showed up, she thought. She put a stack of books down on the counter.

"You planning on doing a little light reading?" Luis asked, raising his eyebrows.

"They're for Lira. She gave me this big list of books to get her from the library." She sat down at the counter. "I don't know how the hell she thinks she's going to read all these at once, but right now, I'm gonna get her whatever she asks for. She could tell me she wanted a pet camel and I'd probably go straight to Egypt and get her one."

"Don't tell her that," warned Becky. "She might ask for a ring."

"Well, she'll end up getting one of those even if she doesn't ask." Amy rubbed the tired muscles in her face and then looked up to see her mother and Luis gaping at her. "What?"

"You're proposing to Lira?" asked Luis.

"Well, not right *now*. I don't have a ring. I don't even have a plan. But I decided at the hospital that, when she's better and we're not in the middle of a crisis anymore, I'm gonna ask her to marry me. I think she deserves that, and I want to be with her for the rest of my life anyway, so what could it hurt to make it official?" She looked from Becky to Luis. "Do you guys not think she'll say yes?"

"Oh no, she'll say yes," Becky assured her. "I see the way she looks at you and talks about you. You're her Princess Charming. I just didn't know *you* were thinking about marriage."

Luis started snickering. "*What* is so funny?" Amy demanded, scowling.

"I'm sorry. I just can't picture you being any kind of princess."

Amy cuffed him on the back of the head. "I'm going to need a lot of time to plan things out, anyway. I have to get a ring, and any ring that would be worthy of her would probably be out of my price range, so I don't know what to do about that. And I have to come up with some creative and memorable way to propose, because she loves all that romantic crap. But all *I* have to plan is the proposal, right? I'm sure she'll plan the wedding. I mean, if it were up to me, we'd just sneak to a courthouse and get married in our regular clothes, but she'll never go for that. She'll want a big wedding with everyone we know, and a nice reception, and a fancy dress..." She looked up at her mother, reality sinking in. "She's probably going to make *me* wear a wedding dress."

Luis snickered again. "I think Ellen DeGeneres got married in a suit. I saw it on the cover of a magazine."

"I would actually do that, but I don't think Lira will let me. Every time we go somewhere nice, she wants me to put on a dress. She thinks I look *pretty*."

"You *do* look pretty when you fix yourself up," agreed Becky. "Don't worry, me and Lira will find you the perfect dress."

"I hate it when you two gang up on me," Amy grumbled. Luis was still snickering. Amy rounded on him. "Stop laughing at my hypothetical future wedding and tell me about the case. Do you have anything new?"

"What case?" Becky asked them. "I thought your case was closed. The man's dead, isn't he?"

"He's dead," Luis assured her. "He just may have had a

friend, or a rival. It's not exactly *our* case anyway, since he didn't kill in our jurisdiction, but we're working with other jurisdictions to help solve it." He turned to Amy. "So, our other killer isn't in the habit of taking his victims home with him. He rapes them, kills them, and dumps the body, all in one night. He has a much longer list of victims than Nielson has, but Nielson did a lot more to each victim, so it's kind of a tossup. In a sense, the other guy's body count *is* his tally, so we're theorizing that Nielson was doing the literal tally marks as a way of letting him know that he was just as prolific, maybe more so, in his own way."

"I hate them both," said Amy. "But they must have known each other personally. Why else would he care what the other guy thinks?"

"No, there has to be some connection," agreed Luis.

"But we only found Nielson's DNA on our victims, right?"

"Yes. You definitely shot the right person, and it does look like he was working alone. And, so far, we still have no reason to believe his acquaintance is going to pose a threat to you or Lira. But we'll keep the squad car outside just in case."

"I knew it!" exclaimed Becky. "I knew something wasn't right! When I got here I saw this man sitting in his car down the street, and I could swear he was looking at me. Why don't they park closer to the house, though?"

"Keep your voice down," said Amy. "We told them to stay down the block so they would be less noticeable. Lira doesn't know about this other killer, and she doesn't need to know. She's nervous enough as it is."

"It's just a precaution," Luis assured Becky. "Just until the guy is caught."

"They better catch him soon," said Becky. "My poor daughter-in-law needs to be able to move on with her life. We have a wedding to plan if we can ever get all this behind us."

Amy had to smile. Luis was looking at her very seriously, though.

"Amy, it's been almost a week since we found Lira," he pointed out. "You can't keep putting off her victim statement.

Please bring her in tomorrow so we can get his over with."

Amy bristled. "She had her first therapy session yesterday, and she had to relive the whole thing there. I don't want to make her do it again so soon."

"You know if it was anyone else you would be chomping at the bit to get them to talk so you could get the information you needed."

"But it's not anyone else. It's not even my case anymore. My only job right now is taking care of Lira."

"Which is why you need to make sure we catch the man who's still out there, who could still hurt her."

"She doesn't know anything about him. She can't tell you anything helpful."

"We still need her statement. You *know* that, Amy. We can make it as easy on her as possible. I'll be there, and someone from Sex Crimes will be there."

"*Not* Mitch. He's not going anywhere near her."

"Of course not Mitch. But Mitch's new partner, Allison Sims, is really great with victims. I think Lira will feel comfortable with her. And you can come with her, to help keep her calm. You just can't be part of the questioning process."

"Can't it wait?" asked Becky, pulling her casserole out of the oven. "The poor girl's been through hell. Like Amy said, she's nervous. She doesn't really want to be around people much right now. She just wants Amy."

"It really can't wait," insisted Luis. "We should have already done it. We need to talk to her while it's still fresh on her mind. You know that, Amy."

"I'll talk to her about it," Amy promised him. "But I'm not making her do anything she doesn't want to do. And I don't want her to know about that other guy. I don't think she can handle it right now."

"I'll make sure the interview is conducted in such a way that she doesn't know there's another perp. We have to ask her if she saw or heard about anybody else, but we would ask that anyway, just to be sure."

"Are you staying for dinner?" Becky asked Luis. "It's chicken and dumplings casserole. One of Lira's favorites."

"Thanks, Mrs. Sadler, but I have to get home." He looked at Amy before going out the door. "I'll call you tomorrow about that statement."

"You should see if Lira's awake, and bring her down to eat if she is," Becky suggested when he was gone.

"I'll check on her," said Amy. "But you know she isn't going to eat."

"She has to start sometime."

"I hope." She sighed in frustration. "Usually I'm the one who doesn't eat enough under stress. I've seen Lira eat a whole box of cookies after a bad day."

"Well, she's never been under this kind of stress before."

"I know. It makes me so mad. Basically, that son of a bitch took her away from me, and I got her back, but she's not the same anymore. It's not fair."

"She'll be the same again. Just give her time. I think she's doing pretty well, given the circumstances."

"She is, and I'm really proud of her, but I want my happy Lira back." She closed her eyes, trying to keep the tears in. "If he were still alive, I'd give *him* a tally mark for every tear she's shed because of him, and every meal she's skipped, and every nightmare she's had."

"Enough violent talk." Becky put her hand over Amy's. "You need to stop focusing on what he took from you and start focusing on what you still have. Upstairs is a very strong woman who loves you enough to get up every morning and keep trying, even though some days I'm sure it would be easier to just pull the blankets over her head. She's trying twice as hard as she would just for herself, because she knows it's breaking your heart to see her like this."

"I know." She wiped her eyes.

"And about the ring. I know you're worried about not being able to afford a nice one, but what about a family heirloom?"

"What do you mean? Dad never gave you an engagement ring."

"I've had my grandmother's engagement ring in a safety deposit box ever since she died. I haven't looked at it in years, but I always thought it was pretty. It had an emerald in the middle, with little diamonds around it in a kinda fancy design. I never had it appraised, but it could be worth something, and at least it has a family connection. She might like that."

Amy was touched. "You would actually give it to me?"

"Well, I'd always hoped I could give it to your brother someday to propose with, but you're the one looking for a ring, and I think I'd like Lira to have it. You could take it to a jeweler, get it cleaned up and resized."

"That sounds really nice, Mom. I'd have to look at it first though, to decide if it's something she'd want."

"I'll get it from the bank tomorrow so you can see it. Now go get Lira. You know she'll have to eat at least a little of my chicken and dumplings."

Chapter 20

Lira nervously eyed the police station as Amy parked the car. She'd never felt this kind of trepidation when coming here before. This was a familiar place. She came here all the time to see Amy.

Except this was her first time coming here as a victim.

Her heart rate sped up as she thought of the story she was going to have to tell inside. She looked around frantically, remembering the simple grounding technique her therapist had taught her in their first session. She started working through her senses. What could she see? Her eyes landed on the tree in front of the station. It didn't have leaves yet, but spring was almost here, and the buds looked ready to burst. It would have them soon. And she could hear birds singing, because the songbirds were coming back. That was good. Lira loved this time of year.

Amy came around the car and opened Lira's door, helping her out. Lira inhaled deeply. It was starting to smell like spring outside. It had rained early this morning, and the scent was still in the air. *Petrichor.* That was the name of the smell. She wondered if Amy knew that. She concentrated on the feeling of the ground beneath her feet, of Amy's hand on her back, as she walked into the building. It was okay. She was safe here.

Amy led her onto the elevator, up to the Sex Crimes Unit where she used to work. A tall, slender woman with chin-length brown hair met them in the hall. "You must be Lira," she said. "I'm Detective Alison Sims from Sex Crimes. I don't think we've met." She held out her hand to shake, but then dropped it again when she noticed Lira's cast.

"It's good to meet you," Lira said quietly. Alison seemed nice, and they would probably work together sometime. She wished she could have met her under different circumstances though.

"If you're ready, we can go ahead and get this over with," said Alison, leading them down the hall. "Detective Martinez is waiting for us in the interview room. We're going to use the video suite."

Lira looked uncertainly at Amy. "It's standard procedure with sexual assault victims," Amy explained.

Lira nodded and started down the hall. A wave of nausea swept over her as she thought about having to be filmed talking about the horrible things that had happened to her. "Petrichor," she said suddenly, looking urgently at her girlfriend.

Amy frowned. "What?"

"Petrichor. It's the scent in the air after rain, when there's been a dry spell. It's a combination of plant oils and chemicals from bacteria in the soil."

"Okay. Good to know."

"I like it. I like the way it smells."

Amy kissed her cheek. "Of course you do."

They walked into the interview room. Lira had never been in one of these before. There wasn't much to look at in here. Plain walls, a table with two chairs on each side, a mirror that she knew was also a window. Luis was sitting at the table, and he smiled when he saw her. She tried to smile back, but found herself shrinking against Amy instead.

"It's okay," Amy murmured in her ear. "I'm going to stay with you the whole time."

"You can sit down," Alison said, taking the seat next to Luis. Lira and Amy sat across from them.

"The way this works is, you can take a break any time you want," Alison explained. "Amy can stay as long as that makes you feel better, but if you decide at any point you'd like her to step out, then she will."

"Likewise, if you decide you don't want a man in the room, I can leave," said Luis. "I'm here because we're putting a homicide case to rest, but it's also a sex crimes case. Alison can do the interview by herself if you'd prefer."

Lira thought she might prefer that, but she hated to say so. Luis was Amy's partner, their friend. She couldn't just kick him out.

"We need you to share all the details you can remember, whether you think they're significant or not," said Alison, looking through a file folder. "When you're ready, you can start at the beginning."

"Which is the beginning?" asked Lira. "The beginning of the case, or the beginning of what happened to me?"

"I've read all your notes about the autopsies. Are there other details that aren't in your notes?"

Lira shook her head. "No, that should be everything."

"Then why don't we start with the day you were taken."

Lira shuddered, reaching for Amy's hand. "I, um...well, I went home on my lunch break that day. Normally I have lunch with Amy when we both can, but she was on the other side of town doing interviews and she texted me that she wasn't going to make it. So I went home and made a sandwich, and I let the dog out and played with the cat. Then when it was time to go back, I let the dog in and I went out the back door. I turned around to lock it and then I felt someone grab me from behind and put his hand over my mouth and stick a needle in my arm."

"Were you aware that anyone had followed you?"

"No. If I'd known, I would have called Amy." She felt a little panicked. *Should* she have known? Was it her fault this happened?

"They have to ask," Amy told her gently. "Sometimes people notice things, but don't realize their significance until later."

Lira nodded. "I didn't notice anything out of the ordinary. I was really happy. I was looking forward to seeing Amy later."

"So what happened after he grabbed you?"

"I tried to get away, but then I blacked out. When I woke up again, I was in his house. I was in a bed, and I didn't have any clothes on, and I had a cut on my chest that was bleeding. A tally mark." She gripped Amy's hand tighter, looking down at the table. "And I knew...I knew I had been raped."

"How did you know?"

"I...was in pain. A lot of pain. My..." She looked at Luis self-consciously. She was a doctor. She was used to discussing the intimate details of people's bodies with others, including Luis. It usually didn't bother her at all. But this was different. This was *her* body.

"Maybe I'll just step out for a bit," said Luis, getting up. Lira felt bad, but she let him go. She knew he was probably just going to go into the other room where he could listen, but that was better than looking at his face.

"So what did you do when you woke up?"

"Well, I knew he had to be the killer we were looking for, so I was really scared. I looked around for a way out and I saw a window across the room, so I got up to run over there and call for help, but I fell down. My ankle was chained to the bed. I should have expected that, but I forgot. I landed really hard on my knee and then I heard him coming upstairs, so I got back on the bed and pulled the blanket over me."

"So then you saw him?"

Lira nodded.

"What did he look like?"

Lira tried to pull the image into her mind. "He was big. I think he had blond hair."

"Can you describe his face?"

She shook her head. "I don't remember it."

"You never saw it?"

"I did, but I can't remember." She could see his outline in her mind, but there were just shadows where his face should be.

"Okay, let me see if you can ID him from a picture." Alison took four pictures out of a folder and lay them in front of her. Lira scanned each one. The first man had dark hair. The second was blond, but too skinny. When she saw the third, she gasped.

"That's him," she said, pointing.

"You're sure?"

"Yes. Please put it away." She could see it now, in her mind: his face, as he studied her, staring unabashedly at her body when he pulled the blanket off. She could hear his breathing too. He sounded thoughtful, excited. He was excited about *her*, about what he was going to do to her, but she didn't want to be there. She squirmed in her seat, turning toward Amy, who put an arm around her shoulders.

"We can take a break if you want," Amy told her.

Lira shook her head. "No. Let's keep going." She wanted nothing more than to leave this room, but she knew once she left, she'd never be able to bring herself to come back in. *Ground yourself. What do you see?* The room was so blank, so featureless. She looked at Amy, beautiful Amy with her unkempt hair and her kind hazel eyes. Amy was there. She was real. She had to focus on her.

"Okay, so when he came upstairs, what happened?"

"He had a camera. He wanted to take my picture to send to the police, like he did with the others. I wouldn't look at the camera though, but he took it anyway. And then he asked me who Amy was. He said I kept saying her name earlier, but I didn't remember. I said she's my girlfriend. I wasn't thinking. I just answered the question. He asked if she was Amy Sadler, the detective on his case, and I said yes, and then he asked why I called for her and I said because she loves me. She wouldn't let anyone hurt me. So he said he'd send the picture to her." Lira began to cry.

"Sweetie, why don't we go just take a rest?" Amy asked her. "We don't have to do this all at once."

"No, I want to," insisted Lira. "After he took my picture, he brought me some food and water and then left again for a while. I tried to find a way out, but I couldn't get out of the handcuffs, and there was no way to get the handcuffs off the bed. I couldn't get to the window. So I made a plan that when he came back, if he tried to inject me again I was going to try to inject him instead. Then maybe I would find a phone in his pocket and I could call for help. When he did come back, he had a syringe so I tried really hard to overpower him. I fought him for a few minutes but then he grabbed my wrist and twisted it until the bones popped, and it hurt so much I just froze and he injected me. So I blacked out again and when I woke up, I had another tally mark and he was still there, getting dressed. He got mad because I had never eaten the food. He said I had to eat it so I tried, but I felt so sick I just threw it back up and then he got even madder and he hit me and he brought me paper towels and a trash can and said I had to clean it up. So I did my best, but it was hard because I only had my left hand and I was shaking so hard." She was shaking now, she realized. She could still see the interview room, but she also saw the bedroom he had kept her in. She tried to ground herself more fully in this room, but it wasn't working. All she heard was the sound of her own crying, and that was in both places.

"Do you remember him saying anything else?" Alison asked gently.

"No," said Lira. "I…it kind of runs together after that. I lost track of time, and I saw some things that weren't real. I saw Amy come to get me, but when I tried to touch her, she wasn't there. He kept coming back and hurting me and I tried to fight him, but he was stronger and he would always give me the injection, and then I would just sleep. Every time I woke up, the pain was worse than before. Usually I was alone except when he brought me food or when he wanted to…to inject me again. I tried reasoning with him once, to humanize myself. I told him about my pets and my house and my family, but he never said anything back. He acted like he couldn't hear me anymore. He didn't talk to me much at all. I only tried to eat one other time and I threw up again and he hit me again, so I was scared to try anymore after that. Then he brought me water and pills. He said the pills would make me sleep longer and when I woke up, he would have a surprise for me. I wouldn't take them so finally he pushed them into my mouth and held me down until I swallowed them. Then I went to sleep, and when I woke up I was in the hospital with Amy." She looked at Amy, who had been gently rubbing her back as she spoke, and saw tears running down her face. "Are you okay?" she asked her.

"Me?" said Amy in surprise. "I'm all right. Are *you* okay?"

Lira wasn't sure. She kept seeing his face, now that she had seen his picture. He was taking up all her senses again. She could see the way he looked at her, hear his breathing, feel his hands on her, smell his sweat.

"Lira," said Alison. "Can you confirm that he was the only person there with you?"

"Y-yes. It was just him and me in the house."

"No visitors?"

"No."

"Did you ever hear him talking on the phone, or talking about anyone?"

"No, never." Lira looked around, but all she could see was the bedroom where she had been held captive. She could feel the cold air hitting her skin as he pulled the blanket from her and stared down at her naked body, breathing heavily, the syringe in his hand. She wanted to tell him just to get it over with and leave her, but he liked to drag it out, to lightly touch her skin while she curled into a ball, protecting herself as much as she could. "Please stop," she said quietly, plaintively. "Please stop."

"You want to stop the interview?" Alison asked, looking confused.

"I want...I want him to stop hurting me."

"Baby, he can't hurt you anymore," Amy assured her. "He's dead. I made sure of it. He'll never touch you or anyone else ever again."

"But...it still...hurts. It still hurts. I still feel it."

"We're done here," said Amy firmly, helping Lira from her chair and guiding her from the room. Alison didn't bother to argue.

Chapter 21

A week after Lira was released from the hospital, Amy brought her to the doctor's office for her scheduled follow-up appointment. She knew this would involve a gynecological exam to make sure her stitches were healing properly, which was not going to be pleasant. To make matters worse, Lira's regular doctor was on vacation, so Amy had to make the appointment with someone she was unfamiliar with.

Amy chatted with Lira while she waited, sheet wrapped around her waist, for the doctor to come in. She did her best to keep the conversation light, to take Lira's mind off the situation as much as possible. Lira was doing her best to be brave, and she *was* brave. She was the bravest person Amy knew. From her years in Sex Crimes, Amy knew it was kind of a big deal that Lira was at this follow-up appointment. Most rape victims never made it to their follow-ups, if they even got them scheduled. They would panic over the thought of someone touching them, or decide they couldn't talk about the rape at all anymore and just wanted to move on, or would forget – literally forget – that they had an appointment scheduled. The stress of rape was so overwhelming that you never really knew how a victim would behave from one day to the next, and this often made it extremely difficult to catch the perp or to prosecute. Amy had often taken it upon herself to call victims and remind them of appointments, even drive them if necessary, anything to make sure they got what they needed and didn't give up on going after the rapist. She'd never actually attended one of these appointments though, had never imagined having to do so for the love of her life one day.

It was hard to believe that just two weeks ago, Lira was still her usual joyful self. Now she seemed to have drawn in on herself.

She was sitting now in what had become her usual posture: shoulders hunched forward, eyes downcast (but frequently darting upwards as if checking for potential threats), broken wrist held protectively against her chest. It wasn't fair that someone could do this to her in a matter of days. Her beautiful green eyes, normally inquisitive and full of wonder, were now filled with fear, pain, bewilderment. Of *course* she was bewildered. She had put nothing but love and beauty into the world, and she had gotten the exact opposite in return. *Never again*, Amy promised herself. She would make sure that Lira got only what she deserved for the rest of her life.

The doctor finally came in, a youngish blonde woman who introduced herself as Dr. Peterson.

"I read over your notes from the hospital," she said, professionally but not as gently as Amy would have liked. "So you had some vaginal tearing that had to be stitched?"

"Yes," said Lira quietly.

Dr. Peterson looked through the notes on her laptop. "And you've already been tested for sexually transmitted infections."

"Yes, and the…the man who attacked me was tested in autopsy as well. Everything came back negative."

"That's good. And you took emergency contraception within the right time frame?"

"Yes."

"Then you're not too likely to be pregnant, but we can do a test just to make sure. We could do that today, or we could wait another week."

"I'll wait," said Lira.

"Okay. How are you feeling? Are you in any pain?"

Lira nodded.

"What hurts?"

"Everything," said Lira, her voice barely audible. "Everything hurts."

"Just a general ache all over?"

Lira nodded again.

"What does that mean?" asked Amy in alarm. She knew Lira was in pain, but she hadn't realized *everything* hurt.

"It's most likely muscle tension, from stress. How are you sleeping?"

"Not well," Lira admitted. "I'm having a lot of nightmares."

"Are you eating okay?"

Lira shifted uncomfortably. "Not really."

"She's *not* eating," Amy cut in, gently running her fingers through Lira's hair as they talked. "Just a few bites here and there is all we can get down her."

"I don't have any appetite," said Lira. "And when I try to eat, it turns my stomach."

"It's not unusual," Dr. Peterson assured them. "Are you having any other problems? Difficulty concentrating, crying more than usual, startling easily?"

"All of those."

"Are you having a lot of flashbacks?"

Lira nodded. "But I'm learning how to manage them."

"Yes, your notes said you were in counseling. Have you had any thoughts of suicide?"

Amy froze and looked at her girlfriend. "No," said Lira. Amy breathed a sigh of relief.

Dr. Peterson typed something into the computer. "The way you're feeling right now is normal, but antidepressants would lessen a lot of those symptoms. I could start you on 20 milligrams of fluoxetine daily. It would cut down on the flashbacks and nightmares, make you less jumpy."

"How long would she have to take it?" asked Amy. She wanted Lira to have whatever would help her to feel better, but she hated for her to be stuck on antidepressants forever because of what some asshole did to her.

"Generally six months to a year, but it depends on how she does," said Dr. Peterson. "If she sticks with the counseling, that will also help a lot. Do you want me to write you a prescription?"

Lira nodded. "That would probably be best." Her voice sounded tired, resigned.

Dr. Peterson sent away the prescription on her computer and then wheeled her chair over for Lira's exam.

"Scoot down and put your feet in the stirrups," she instructed. Lira did as she was told, her fingers tightening around Amy's hand. She was shaking, and Amy wondered if it would be possible to do the exam without hurting her even worse.

Dr. Peterson picked up the speculum. "Okay, I'm just going to touch you."

"No." Lira suddenly recoiled, pulling her feet back out of the stirrups and reaching for Amy. "Please don't."

"Hey. It's okay, baby." Amy wrapped her arms around Lira, holding her trembling body close. She knew Lira's instinctive need to protect herself outweighed her logic right now, and it was hard seeing her like this.

Dr. Peterson did not look pleased. "Dr. Ward, I know this is uncomfortable, but I need to make sure you're healing properly and that there's no sign of infection."

"I'm...I'm still very sore," Lira told her, trying to sound reasonable.

"She's already on antibiotics," Amy pointed out. "So it's not very likely she'd get an infection, is it?"

"I need to check to be sure, and to make sure everything's

healing okay and that nothing is wrong with the stitches."

"I can't," Lira said, shaking her head. "It hurts too much."

"Can't this wait until she's in a little less pain?" Amy asked. She knew it should be done, but she couldn't stand to make Lira go through this when she was so frightened. And she didn't even like to think about how much it might hurt. When she first came home from the hospital, Lira hadn't even been able to sit without a cushion. Sticking something in there right now was *not* going to feel good.

"It would be best if we could do it now." Dr. Peterson looked at Lira. "Dr. Ward, you understand why I need to examine you, right?"

Lira nodded, clearly struggling with herself. She *wanted* to be reasonable. She *wanted* to do what was medically necessary. But lately she had been reduced to this, this almost animalistic need to protect herself from pain at all costs.

Reason seemed to win, and Lira slowly scooted back down on the table, putting her feet in the stirrups. Dr. Peterson approached with the speculum again.

"*No!*" Lira screamed at the last second, pulling her feet from the stirrups and pressing her knees together. "I can't do it. I can't." She looked up at Amy, tears running down her face.

Dr. Peterson gave Amy an exasperated look. What the fuck did she expect her to do, hold Lira down so she could do the exam? *That* sure as hell wasn't happening.

"You can't make her do this if she doesn't want to," said Amy quietly, gathering Lira in her arms.

"I am aware of that, but it really is in her best interest to go ahead. If you could perhaps encourage her—"

"I want her to have the medical treatment she needs. I really do. But I have to take her emotional well-being into account as well, and this—" Amy motioned to the exam table, to the speculum in the doctor's hands— "clearly isn't good for her right now."

Dr. Peterson sighed in resignation. "I can write her a prescription for Valium. When you leave, go to the front desk and make another appointment, preferably within the next few days. About an hour before that appointment, she should take the Valium. Hopefully it will relax her enough for her to be able to get through the exam."

Amy nodded. She didn't like the thought of drugging Lira for this, but if it was the only way to get her through it, then it was what they would have to do. "Is that what you want to do?" she asked Lira, tenderly tucking a strand of hair behind her ear.

Lira shook her head. "I don't want to come back. I can do this." She slowly let go of Amy and got into position for the third time. Dr. Peterson cautiously approached, but Lira didn't react. In fact, her muscles were no longer tensed, and her eyes had lost their focus. She was dissociating, Amy realized. She wasn't even here.

Dr. Peterson didn't seem to notice. She completed the exam, said everything was healing as it should, and left them alone. Amy had to say Lira's name repeatedly to get her back to planet Earth so she could help her get dressed.

When they got home, Lira went upstairs to lie down, clearly exhausted from her ordeal. Amy went into the kitchen, let the dog out, and started to load the dishwasher, but she broke down crying. She leaned over the cabinet, shoulders shaking, until she heard a knock at the door. She composed herself as much as she could and went to see who it was, opening the door to her mother.

"Amy, sweetheart, you've been crying," said Becky as she came in.

"Lira had a hard time at her appointment. Didn't want to be touched."

"Did they say she's okay, at least?"

"Yeah, she's healing fine. She's resting now."

"Well, I brought you something." Becky reached into her purse and produced a small box. "This isn't the original box, but here's my grandmother's ring."

Amy cracked open the box to reveal a silver ring with an emerald in the middle, surrounded by an intricate design with tiny diamonds. "It's beautiful," she said.

"I think it would look perfect on your Lira," said Becky.

Amy smiled. "It would look amazing on her. I hope she'll want it. I mean, I hope she'll want *me*."

"Of course she will. Don't be ridiculous. I'd get it professionally cleaned if I were you, and you'll need to figure out her ring size so it can be made to fit her."

"Yeah. I've got time. She's in no condition to be thinking about weddings right now." Amy wrapped her mother in a hug. "Thank you for this, and for everything you've done for Lira."

"You don't need to thank me," chuckled Becky. "I love her too."

***

After finding a safe hiding place for the ring, Amy went upstairs to check on Lira. She found her curled up in bed, but not sleeping.

"Hey." Amy sat down on her side of the bed and moved Lira's hair out of her face. "How are you feeling?"

"Kind of sore. She did the exam, didn't she?"

Amy's heart seized. "The pelvic exam? Yeah, she did it. Don't you remember?"

"Not really." Lira rubbed one eye, then the other with her left hand. "What did she say?"

"She said everything's healing like it's supposed to."

"That's good." Lira reached for Amy's hand, twining their fingers together. "What if it turns out I *am* pregnant?"

"Well, that's not very likely, is it? You took the emergency contraception they gave you at the hospital."

"I'll feel better when I'm sure. Emergency contraception doesn't work in at least eleven percent of cases."

"Which means it does work the other eighty-nine percent of the time, and that's if you even needed it. You would have had to be ovulating at the exact wrong moment to even have a chance of getting pregnant. So you're worried about something that's a longshot, which is exactly what you always tell me not to do."

"I know." Lira sat up and looked at Amy miserably. "But what would we do, if I was?"

"I really think that would have to be your decision. But I would support whatever you decided."

"What if I wanted to terminate?"

"Then I would take you to the clinic and hold your hand during the procedure. If you don't want any part of that bastard living inside of you, I can't really blame you for that."

Lira nodded as if taking this in. "And what if I wanted to keep it?"

"Then we'd have a baby."

"You would be okay with that?"

"We've tossed around the idea of maybe having one someday. So we didn't want one now, and certainly not like this, but things don't always happen the way you plan. And we *would* save a lot of money on sperm."

"Wouldn't you worry that the child might have inherited violent tendencies from the biological father?"

"Nah. We don't even know who your father is, but there has to be a reason why your mom doesn't want to talk about him, and yet, look how you turned out. I bet the kid would be sweet and smart and beautiful, just like you."

"I think I would worry. But I'm not sure I could terminate either." She lay back down, looking defeated. "I just need to not be pregnant."

"Why did you decide to wait about taking the test?"

"If I were pregnant, it's possible my hCG levels wouldn't be high enough yet to show it. I could test negative and find out later I *was* pregnant. I'd rather wait a few more days so I can be certain the results are accurate."

"That makes sense. In the meantime, you just need to focus on taking care of yourself." She leaned down to kiss Lira on the head. Lira's eyes moved to Amy's face with a look that said she wanted more, so Amy leaned back down and kissed her lips, letting Lira decide how long the kiss would last.

"I love you," Lira said softly when she finally broke the kiss.

"I love you too, gorgeous lady. And as much as it breaks my heart to see you this sad, every time I look at you I still can't help feeling overjoyed that you're back here with me, where you belong."

Lira smiled slightly. "That makes me a little less sad."

Amy kissed her again. "What would you like for dinner? Tell me anything you think you can eat more than a few bites of, and I'll get it for you."

Lira thought for a minute. "Could you make me a Belgian waffle?"

"Well, we have the mix, and I'm sure I could figure out how to work your waffle iron."

"Could you put strawberries on it?"

"I could. I'll go down and make it for you, okay? I'll call you when it's ready." She gave Lira one last kiss before getting up and heading downstairs, thinking to herself, *he damn well better not have made her pregnant*. She was telling the truth when she said she'd raise the kid if it came to that, but the asshole had already rearranged Lira's life far more than he had any right to, and it was clear that trying to make a decision about it was going to break Lira down even more. Besides, it sounded too much like another stupid fairy tale scenario. *If a demon impregnates an angel*, she mused, *what is the result?*

Chapter 22

"Do you think we could go on a vacation sometime soon?" Lira asked. She was sitting on the couch with her laptop and Amy was beside her, supposedly watching TV, but Lira could see that her eyes weren't focused. Amy couldn't seem to focus on anything anymore, and Lira knew it was because she was worried about her. Everyone was. They all gave her the same look, a look that said, "I can't believe this happened to you." She didn't fault them for it. She still felt like she was trying to wake up from a nightmare, that the past few weeks couldn't have been real. But she was so tired of feeling like she was attending her own funeral. She needed people to stop grieving over her, but how? Maybe she *wasn't* really here anymore. She was healing physically at least. Her bruises were going away, her cuts mending, and she knew now that she wasn't pregnant. She kept trying to do normal things again, at least around the house, but she would find herself just staring into space and suddenly realize that a lot of time had passed. It was hard for her to even imagine getting back to work and other social obligations when she was like this.

"A vacation?" Amy turned from the TV to look at her.

"Yeah, someplace warm."

"Sure, that sounds nice. We might as well spend the money your mom keeps wiring you to 'aid in your recovery.'"

"Good, because I've always wanted to stay in one of those jungle treehouses."

"Wait, hang on, *what*?"

"There are hotels that have treehouses you can stay in. I'll show you." She started typing one-handedly on her laptop.

"You'd actually want to sleep in a treehouse? Like, *overnight*?"

"It's not like a kid's treehouse." She turned her computer to show Amy a picture. "They're fully enclosed, and they have electricity and bathrooms. They have the same furniture as any hotel room, but they're up in the trees, and you get a private deck where you can sit and look at the wildlife."

"But the door locks and everything?"

"Of course! This one is in Costa Rica, right next to a wildlife preserve. From the treehouse you can see all kinds of hummingbirds, and other animals like sloths and iguanas."

"Well, you know how much I love iguanas."

Lira sensed Amy's sarcasm, but she chose to ignore it. "There's a beach nearby. And an active volcano."

"Who doesn't want to be near an active volcano?"

"And there's a spa at the hotel! We can get massages and skin treatments."

Amy gave her a tired smile. "If you think you'd enjoy sleeping in a treehouse surrounded by iguanas, then book us one. It might be good for us to get away for a while. Especially you, since you've hardly been out of the house."

"I want my wrist to get better first, though." She looked down at her cast, which was now a riot of color. Everyone who'd come to see her had added a note or doodle with Amy's markers. Most of those visitors had stopped coming after the first week, but Luis still dropped by to see Amy, and Clarissa came to see Lira and update her on what was happening in the morgue. And, of course, Becky came by every single day to check on them both.

"Well, I doubt they have treehouses available for next week anyway." Amy stretched and put her arm around Lira's waist. "We have plenty of vacation time though. It would just be nice if you'd start eating first so you can actually enjoy the local cuisine on our trip."

Lira put her laptop down. "I want to, but I'm just not hungry."

"Have you talked to your therapist about that?"

"She said it was normal. It'll get better, especially once the antidepressants have had time to take effect."

"How long will that take?"

"It can take several weeks to really feel the effects, but spending time in nature can also decrease feelings of stress and depression, so visiting the rainforest might give me a boost as well."

"We should *definitely* go then." Amy gently fingered Lira's hair. "You know I don't have much appetite when I'm under a lot of stress, but you and Mom make me eat anyway, and I'm always glad."

"I'll keep trying."

Amy hugged her. "I don't mean to pressure you. I just don't want you to get sick."

"I know." Lira leaned against Amy, thinking about how hard this must be for her. Not only had someone she loved gotten hurt, but the entire situation must be triggering for her. She'd experienced her own sexual assault once, had gone through many of the same emotions Lira was experiencing now. It had taken her some time to get to a place where the memories of that event didn't affect her daily life anymore, and now she was probably experiencing them all over again. She ran her fingers along Amy's wrist until she felt the subtle bump, the scar from where she'd strained so hard against the rope Flynn had bound her with that it had cut deeply into her skin, and stroked it pensively.

She thought about the last time they'd had sex, the night before her abduction. She tried to remember how it had felt. She didn't know if it was a blessing or a cruel irony that they had had such an exceptional sexual experience the night before their lives were torn apart. She still remembered every detail; she had clung to the memory during her captivity, reminding herself that her body could also feel good. Above all, she liked to remember the feeling of being *cherished*.

She knew Amy still cherished her, in spirit anyway. But she missed being cherished in body as well.

"Why do you keep touching my scar?" Amy asked her.

"I'm reminding myself that it's possible to put traumatic events behind us and not let them rule our lives. When I touch this scar, most of the time I hardly think about how you got it. It's just part of you, and I think it makes you seem stronger." She looked up at Amy. "I hope that's how I can feel one day about my own scars."

"You already seem stronger than ever to me." Amy kissed her.

Lira studied Amy's face. "I want to have sex with you."

Amy's eyes widened. "*Now?*"

"Yes, now. My attacker didn't have any sexually transmitted infections, so it should be safe."

"But, it's only been three weeks. You're still healing."

"Well, my dominant hand isn't usable, and you're definitely *not* touching my vagina right now." She tilted her head. "But my tongue is perfectly healthy, and so is my clitoris."

Amy's face softened. "But are you really sure you're ready?"

"Yes. I'm tired of my body being a crime scene. I'm tired of that...monster being the last person to touch me."

Amy cringed.

"It should be you," Lira said gently. "I want *you* to be the most recent person to touch me. It should *always* be you."

Amy nodded. "I really don't want it to be him anymore."

"So, we can do this?"

"If you're absolutely, one hundred percent sure it's what you want right now. I can wait as long as you need me to."

Lira kissed her. "I'm absolutely, one hundred percent sure it's what I want right now."

Lira thought she should take the lead since Amy seemed nervous. She started to take Amy's shirt off, but it was really hard to do with only one good hand, which was killing the mood a bit.

"Here, I can do that," said Amy. She got up and slowly peeled off her shirt, giving Lira a mock-seductive look as she tossed it aside. She unfastened her bra and made a big show of tossing that down as well. Lira giggled.

"I hope you brought some dollars to put in my G-string," said Amy, unfastening her jeans.

"You don't own a G-string."

"I know, I'm just teasing." Amy cast her jeans aside, leaving only her underwear. "Now I know from past experience that you can get *these* off one-handed," she said, coming closer.

Biting her lip in anticipation, Lira hooked her left thumb over the waistband and tugged Amy's panties down until they dropped to the floor where she could easily step out of them. She gazed up at Amy's naked body admiringly, wishing she could run both hands all over it the way she normally did.

"Okay, I'm all yours," Amy said, reclining on the couch.

"Good." Lira stretched out on top of Amy and kissed her lips, jawline, neck, moving down to admire an exquisite collarbone. She ran the fingers of her left hand along Amy's arm, touching a firm bicep. She loved how strong Amy was, loved that her strength was always protective, never threatening. She realized now how much she missed this, missed being this close to Amy, making her feel good. She loved every contour of Amy's body, and as she reacquainted herself with it, she felt the awakening of real sexual desire in herself; not just the idea of it, but the real thing.

When she finally took Amy into her mouth, she found herself exhaling in pleasure. She loved the taste of her girlfriend. She might never have tasted her again, if the man who'd taken her had gotten his way, so now she savored it, listening to Amy's low moans as she tapped and stroked with her tongue.

Amy must have needed this more than she cared to admit, because it wasn't long at all until she cried out her orgasm. Lira sat up, smiling, and lay back on her end of the couch. "It's my turn now."

Amy moved towards her, hesitantly. "If you change your mind, or you don't like anything I'm doing, just stop me."

"I will, but I'm not—you're not—" She sighed. "You're *you*. I'm not worried."

Amy nodded and gently undressed Lira. There was one horrible moment when Amy lowered her mouth to Lira's breast and Lira involuntarily pulled back, but she begged her not to stop, and Amy listened.

Amy's gentle touch was comforting, but it was harder to receive pleasure than it had been to give it. She didn't feel sexy anymore. She felt like her body was contaminated now, that it was shameful to be seen this way. Logically knowing it wasn't true didn't change the way she felt. Instead she tried to imagine that Amy was making it better, that her loving kisses and caresses were chasing away the ugliness and replacing it with something brand new.

It didn't help that Amy was touching her haltingly, as if she'd never seen a woman's body before. In fact, she was barely touching her at all, gently tracing her fingers over Lira's skin the way she might touch a soap bubble she was trying not to pop.

"Amy," Lira said finally, "I'm not going to break."

"I know, I just...I don't want to hurt you."

"You're not going to hurt me. But I would like it if you did *something* to me."

Amy smiled. "Okay."

"I can get out one of my anatomy books if you need help finding my clitoris."

Amy stifled a laugh. "Did you just make a joke?"

Lira grinned at her. "Yes, I did. You *do* remember where everything is?"

Amy started to laugh for real, and then Lira laughed too. "Yeah," Amy said. "Yeah, I remember."

"Okay then. My clitoris is where I want your tongue, right now."

So Amy obliged, and she didn't hold back so much this time. Lira began to relax more, to focus on her girlfriend instead of on what she was trying to escape from. She could feel Amy's energy, her passion, the restlessness that Lira never understood but loved anyway. And, eventually, she felt her own sweet release.

Afterwards Amy moved to lie down beside her, and Lira wrapped her arms tightly around her girlfriend, holding her close and savoring the feeling of Amy's skin against her own. She wasn't free of pain, but for the first time in weeks, her body actually felt pleasant, loved, not just an object of abuse.

"Thank you," she whispered into Amy's ear.

Chapter 23

Amy woke to a sudden thrashing in the bed beside her. Clea, already getting too familiar with this, jumped down off the foot of the bed.

"No," said Lira softly, and then her voice grew louder. "*No.* Stop, *please*, stop!"

Trust Lira to remember her manners when she's trying to fight off a damn rapist, Amy thought grimly, pushing herself into a sitting position. "Lira," she said loudly. "*Lira*, wake up! You're home. You're safe."

In the dim light from the streetlamp outside, Amy could see Lira's eyes open, but they didn't focus on her.

"Lira, honey, it's me," she said. "Can I touch you now?"

Lira nodded slowly. Amy lay back down and pulled Lira into her arms.

"I remembered something," Lira said softly. "Actually, I don't know if it was a real memory or just a bad dream. But, I can…I can still…feel it." Her breath started coming too fast. She was hyperventilating again.

"Lira, slow down. *Breathe*." Amy rubbed Lira's back slowly. "Think about what's actually around you."

"I can't right now." Lira dissolved into tears and pressed her face against Amy's neck, her shoulders shaking. Amy stroked her hair and tried to be strong for her, but she couldn't this time. She was too tired to make herself stay calm while Lira cried like her heart was being ripped in half. Instead she leaned her face against Lira's hair and cried along with her. *I killed him in real life*, she thought, *but I can't kill him in her mind, and he can still hurt her there.*

They had made love again the previous night, and Lira had insisted on doing the "normal" thing and going to sleep as they were, even though Amy was concerned that the sensation of being naked under a blanket again would trigger more nightmares for Lira. She supposed, though, that the nightmares were going to come either way, and she *was* glad that they had gotten their sex life back, more or less. It wasn't quite the way it used to be. Amy missed being able to just roll over in bed, take Lira in her arms, and make love to her, but with Lira's emotions being all over the map right now, Amy did not feel comfortable initiating. Right now they could have sex only when it was Lira's idea, and Lira had to dictate how it was going to happen.

Still, it was good for them. Lira seemed to be a little happier. She was eating more now. It still wasn't enough, really, but it was a significant improvement over before. Becky was knocking herself out trying to cook Lira's favorite things, to tempt her to eat just a little bit more. Lira also seemed a little less skittish around visitors, and Amy even got her out of the house once to see a movie.

But the nightmares and bad memories still persisted. Amy knew it was normal, but that didn't make it any easier.

Suddenly Lira lifted her head up, wiped Amy's tears away, and kissed her face.

"I really don't deserve you," Amy whispered.

"Why do you keep saying that?"

"Because I don't. Look at you. You've been through the most horrible experience and you're still worried because I'm crying."

Lira seemed a little calmer now. "Well I don't care any less about you just because something bad happened to me. Besides, you're going through something too. You can't make this all about me."

"How is it not about you? You're the one who was kidnapped and…and hurt. And you could have been killed."

"And you're the one who had to look for me, and worry that I was already dead. Honestly, I'm glad if one of us had to be taken by a serial killer that it was me instead of you."

"Really? Every day I wish it had been *me* instead of *you*."

"I'm not surprised. Because in some ways, it's easier to be the one getting hurt than to see someone you love get hurt."

"I guess." She touched Lira's face. "It's the middle of the night, so I'm gonna say something corny, but you can't ever bring it up again."

"Okay."

"You are probably the closest thing to an angel that exists on this Earth. Okay, now forget I said it."

Lira broke into a smile. "I'm really not though."

"Mmm. Ever since this happened, I've been devising forms of torture that I wish I could have inflicted on the man who did this to you. I hate him exactly as much as I love you, but you don't seem to do that. You don't want to torture people. You don't even seem to hate anyone, no matter how much they deserve it."

"Well, I wasn't sad when I found out he died. Actually, I was kind of relieved."

"You'd be crazy if you weren't relieved. But you know, I was going to kill him whether I had to or not. I just wanted him to die for what he did to you."

Lira kissed her. "I know."

"How do you know?"

"Because I know *you*. You would never let anyone by with hurting me. That's why I feel so safe with you."

Amy ran her hand slowly down Lira's back. "You feel tense. Is the dream still bothering you?"

Lira nodded. "I can still feel it."

"What did you remember?"

"I dreamed he was…inside of me." Lira shut her eyes tight. "He wouldn't stop. It felt so real, I thought at first it was a memory coming back, but I couldn't really have stored any memories from when I was unconscious from the ketamine. It was just my brain reconstructing what I know happened. It's just it felt so real, and now the feeling won't go away."

"So do your grounding thing. Go through your senses. What do you feel right now, for real?"

Lira put her head down on Amy's chest and thought. "I can feel you. Your arms around me, and your body under me, and your skin. You're *naked*."

"Yeah, we both are."

Lira ran her fingers along Amy's arm. "You feel warm and safe. And I feel the blankets, and the bed under us. It all feels warm and safe and perfect."

Amy smiled. "Good! Now do another sense. What can you

smell?"

Lira sniffed. "Your hair. I love the smell of your hair." She buried her face against Amy's hair and inhaled.

Amy chuckled. "We can skip sight since it's dark, but what do you hear?"

"I hear cars going by outside. And I hear your voice." She got quiet, but Amy could feel that her breathing had slowed down, and her muscles felt less tense.

"It's funny," Lira remarked. "I used to use dreams to escape from reality, and now I use reality to escape from dreams."

"Your dreams won't always suck this much," Amy promised.

"I know. But my reality now is better than even a good dream."

"Is it? I'm still dreaming about our old reality, before some bastard who didn't even know us decided he had the right to fuck everything up. Doesn't that make you mad?"

"Yes," admitted Lira. "I wish it hadn't happened. I wish things were still the way they were before. But I still feel lucky to be where I am now. I'm alive, I'm safe at home, and I still have you. If things had gone differently—if you hadn't been able to get me when you did—I'd still be there now, going through all that. I'm *very* lucky."

Amy swallowed. "I don't even want to think about you being there that long."

"I can't stop thinking about it," said Lira. "Those other women were each there for a few months, going through the cycle of being drugged and raped over and over, day after day. I never thought about it before, when we were just working the case, but after I was there I realized..." She lifted her head up, peering at Amy through the darkness. "They must have been so *relieved* when he finally killed them."

A chill went down Amy's spine. She thought of their desperate, fruitless attempts to find Jennifer O'Malley and then Rebecca Laurent alive, and wondered how long it took each of them to stop hoping to be saved. Even worse was the thought of Lira eventually wishing for death.

Lira had told Amy, in bits and pieces, much of what happened to her even before making her official victim statement, which filled in the remaining gaps. Amy had replayed it all in her mind so many times, she felt almost like she had been there. She could see it all so clearly: Nielson grabbing Lira from behind and injecting her with ketamine. Lira waking up in that iron bed, ankle cuffed to the frame, and trying to run away, falling down in the process. Lira fighting Nielson, scratching his face, and Nielson breaking her wrist to subdue her. Lira throwing up after trying to eat, and Nielson hitting her as punishment. Lira blacking out repeatedly and waking up each time with a new tally mark carved into her beautiful skin.

The story had been difficult for Amy to listen to, and thinking about it still filled her with a blind rage, but she couldn't stop.

"Amy." Lira's voice brought her back to the present. Amy touched her girlfriend, feeling the silkiness of her hair, trying to push away the pain that had welled up inside.

"Where did you go?" Lira asked her. "You're doing what I do."

"I was just...thinking about everything you told me, about what happened to you."

"So, you're having a flashback about something you weren't even there for?"

"I wouldn't call it a flashback..."

"It affected you like a flashback." Lira put her head back down. "Amy, I still think it would be really helpful if you got counseling too. You went through your own traumatic experience, and now you're taking on the burden of *my* experience as well."

"If you can live through it actually happening to you, I can certainly live through thinking about it."

"I'm living through it with the help of my therapist. And it's actually not unusual for the loved ones of sexual assault survivors to get counseling as well." She kissed Amy tenderly, which was what she tended to do when she really didn't want Amy to argue.

"Okay, I'll think about it," Amy mumbled. "Right now I just want to go back to sleep."

***

Amy was just starting to drift off when she heard a noise outside. She sat up in bed and listened carefully. Yes, there it was again: the crunching of dead leaves. Someone was walking around outside the house, in their side yard. Looking for a way in, perhaps?

She eased herself out from under Lira's arm and went to the window, but she couldn't see a damn thing in the darkness. She would have to go out to investigate. She threw on pants and a t-shirt, grabbed her weapon and a flashlight, and reluctantly woke Lira.

"Baby, I heard something outside, I'm just going to go see what it was," she told her as calmly as she could, thrusting her phone into Lira's hands. "If you hear a gunshot, or if I don't come back, call Luis."

"You think someone's out there?" Lira asked, shivering.

"I'm just gonna make sure. Wake Henry up. I know he's docile, but I like to think he'd defend you if it came to that." She pressed a quick kiss to Lira's brow and hurried downstairs.

She paused in the hallway and listened. She heard the crunching sound again, moving towards the back of the house. She went to the back door, heart pounding. A large part of her hoped it *was* the son of a bitch they were looking for so she could go ahead and take care of him. She wasn't allowed to work the case, of course, but Luis had kept her informed (although he wasn't strictly supposed to), and she knew they had no suspects yet, but that they were digging into Nielson's past. If he wanted to go ahead and come after them, that was just fine. It would save everyone a lot of trouble.

She went out the back door as quietly as she could and crept to the gate, gun ready, still listening. There was a pause, and then she heard the leaves rustling again, mere feet from where she was standing. She carefully undid the latch on the gate, and in one lightning-fast movement, she threw it open, jumped through it, and pointed her gun with a fierce cry of "Hands where I can see them!"

The beam of her flashlight revealed the glowing eyes of a frightened possum. Wrapped in her tail was a bundle of dead leaves. She'd been rustling around gathering nesting materials.

Amy blew out her breath and went back into the house, carefully locking the gate and door behind her. She found Lira upstairs, fully clothed, kneeling on the floor with her arms around Henry. She was shaking.

"It was just a possum," Amy told her. "I'm so sorry. I shouldn't have scared you like that."

Lira breathed a sigh of relief. "So nobody's out there?"

"No. I'm just getting paranoid." She dropped to her knees, gave Henry a pat for guarding Lira, and pulled Lira into her arms.

"I kept telling myself it couldn't be *him*, because you told me he was dead, and I read the autopsy report," said Lira. "But I still felt like it was him trying to take me back."

"No, baby, that can't happen." Amy ran her fingers through Lira's hair. "It's just a mama possum looking for leaves to line her nest with. I freaked out over nothing. I should have just let you sleep."

Lira smiled sympathetically. "It's okay, you were just trying to protect me. Let's get back in bed."

They both shed their hastily donned clothing and climbed back under the covers. A confused Henry curled back up in his dog bed, while Clea settled herself back down near their feet. Amy sighed wearily as Lira turned to face her, laying her head on her shoulder. She hugged her close.

"You did the same thing after Flynn attacked you," Lira pointed out. "You would jump out of bed, thinking you heard someone trying to get in."

"Yeah. I remember."

"It's like I said: you've been traumatized by this experience too. And you were traumatized once before, so I really worry about you."

"I know." Amy closed her eyes and breathed slowly, trying to slow her heart rate back down.

"I think our trip to Costa Rica will be good for both of us," said Lira before falling asleep.

Amy murmured her agreement, but Lira really had no idea how much Amy was looking forward to going abroad; far, far away from the man Nielson had been "competing" with.

She hoped Lira would never have to know.

Chapter 24

Lira picked at her lunch. She was, as usual, trying to get as much down as she could, for Amy's sake. She found that having food in her stomach did not make her feel sick anymore, but it was still hard to get it down with no appetite. Amy was pacing around the kitchen, texting someone and looking agitated.

"I finally got my period this morning," Lira announced.

"Good," said Amy, still distracted.

Lira frowned. "I already knew I wasn't pregnant, of course, but I still didn't like having my cycle thrown off due to stress. I think I'm on my way to feeling more normal now."

Amy looked up and smiled. "That *is* good news."

Lira smiled back. "I was quite relieved that I wasn't pregnant, but it really did make me think about what it would be like to have a baby under better circumstances. Do you think we should, someday?"

Amy was looking at her phone again and clearly not paying attention. "Yeah sure, if you want."

"Whom are you texting?" Lira asked her.

"Just Luis."

"Is he telling you about a case? What are they working on?"

"He's been updating me about cases since I've been gone." She put down the phone. "Are you eating?"

"Yes." Lira dutifully took another bite. She watched Amy stealing glances at her phone, still looking angry. The poor thing had to be going stir crazy by now. They had been off work for a month, which seemed reasonable for Lira, whose scalpel hand was still in a cast, but less so for Amy, who was perfectly healthy.

"Maybe it's time for you to go back to work," Lira suggested. "I can tell you want to, and I'll be okay."

"What? No! I can't just leave you here alone! What if you need to open a jar or something?"

Lira smiled. "Why would I *need* to open a jar while you're gone?"

"Or what if you have a flashback, and you need someone to

call you back to the present?"

"Amy," Lira said softly, "I might have those for the rest of my life. We can't plan around them forever."

"They won't always be as frequent, or as intense. I'm not leaving you. I'll go back when you go back. Besides, we're going to Costa Rica soon. It wouldn't make sense to start working and then leave to go on vacation right away."

"You could fit in two full weeks of work before we go to Costa Rica. I can't work until we get back, and that's if they approve me for light duty while I'm getting the strength back in my wrist. Amy, I really think it would be good for you to get back out in the world and do the job you love. I'll be okay, and you can still check on me during the day. If I really needed you, I'm sure Captain Wheeler and the others would let you go. And then in the evening you can come home and tell me about what you did all day. You can't do that right now. I already know what you did all day. *I was there.*"

Amy looked like she was really considering it. Lira was glad; she knew she'd get lonely being in the house by herself, but she hated knowing she was keeping Amy from doing what she loved most.

Suddenly Amy's face darkened, and she shook her head. "I can't, Lira. Maybe you're ready, but I'm not. I'll go back to work when you go."

Lira's heart sank. "But Amy, there's nothing wrong with you, and you love being a cop—"

"What I love is knowing you're safe. I went through something too, remember? I know three days doesn't sound like much in the grand scheme of things, but it was an eternity for me. I didn't know if I would ever see you again. I felt so helpless knowing what was happening to you and not being able to stop it. And then I got that letter, saying you were calling my name. I know you were drugged and you didn't understand that I couldn't hear you, but I can't get that out of my head. You called for me, and I didn't come."

"But you did come," Lira pointed out, her voice quiet. "You

came *because* I called for you. That was why he sent the letter."

"That's just it." Amy was pacing again. "In the end, that was what saved you. It wasn't me or Luis or any of the good guys. You're here now because he got greedy and decided to take me as well. I didn't protect you, and I didn't save you, but I will be *damned* if I let anyone else touch you as long as I live."

She paused, her eyes meeting Lira's, and that was when something clicked in Lira's head. She'd thought the other night, when Amy had jumped out of bed thinking she heard someone outside, had just been Amy's own post-traumatic stress manifesting itself, but what if there was more to it than that?

"There's something you're not telling me, isn't there?"

Amy looked away.

"Amy." Lira felt cold dread spreading through her chest. "Please tell me."

"It's better if you don't know."

Lira tried to keep her voice steady. "How am I ever going to feel safe if I know you won't tell me when there's a problem?"

Amy gave her an agonized look. "The man who hurt you was, at the time of his death, in contact with someone else who is still out there killing people, someone he was apparently friends with when he was younger, although we can't tell if they were still friends or if they had become enemies. Since we don't know, we're going on the assumption that the surviving killer might target me for killing Nielson, or possibly even you for being the victim that got away. We've had a squad car down the block ever since you got home, and I can't leave you for long periods of time, because that officer is just the backup. I'm the one guarding you."

Lira tried to remember her breathing techniques, but she was drawing a blank. Her breath came faster and faster. She had been calming herself for weeks now by telling herself that she was safe, that the man who took her couldn't hurt her or even think about her anymore. But she wasn't really safe. Everyone had just been letting her think that because they knew she couldn't cope with the truth.

"Lira…" Amy's voice was gentle. "This is why I didn't want

you to know. I didn't want you to be scared when you're trying to get well."

Lira started to cry. "What does he do?"

"What do you mean?"

"The other killer. What does he do to his victims?"

Amy hesitated. "He rapes them and then strangles them."

"Does he drug them?"

"No. He…he doesn't keep them. He kills them after the first time. Why?"

"I just want to know what to expect if he…if he does find me."

"Oh, Lira." Amy came around the counter and took Lira in her arms. "He's not going to find you. They're working very hard on this case, and Luis was just texting me that they just found another victim from the other killer, in Chicago. He's not even in Brookwood, and he's made no effort to contact us, so he probably doesn't even want to find you. But if he did, there's no way in hell any of us are going to let anything happen to you."

Lira heard the logic in her words, but all she could think was, *it's going to happen again, and this time I'll be fully aware while it's happening.*

"I can't do it again," she told Amy. "I can't. This time he would have to kill me, because I can't live through it again. I won't."

"Lira, don't say that." Amy bent down to Lira's eye level. "He *will not* lay a finger on you. It's not like before. We're all coming together to protect you this time, like we should have done in the first place."

"You're sure it's enough?"

"We've got good locks on the doors, I've got my gun, we've got backup outside. You're never alone. We could also have an alarm system put in, if you'd like."

Lira didn't know how to answer. She felt like all the progress she'd made in the past month had just come undone. All of her efforts to ground herself, to work through her feelings, to be intimate with Amy again, to eat—all of it was for nothing if she had to go through the same experience again in the future. She *couldn't,* especially not so soon. She didn't think she would come back from it this time. She pulled back from Amy, trembling violently, and looked at the back door, where she had been taken. If one man could find her at home, so could the other one. He might already know where she lived. His friend could have told him. Maybe he was biding his time, waiting for everyone to think it was safe, before he would come and get her.

"Lira, Lira, I'm so sorry." Amy pulled her close again and kissed her head. "I promise we'll keep you safe. *No one* will hurt you like that again."

"I think I just want to go lie down for a while." Upstairs felt safer than downstairs. She pulled away from Amy, left the remainder of her lunch on the counter, and slowly climbed the stairs, feeling lightheaded. She knew she should be mad at Amy for keeping this secret from her, but she didn't have the energy, and she knew Amy was only trying to protect her. Maybe she was right to do so. After all, Lira had just spent four weeks building up her strength instead of living in fear. But it hurt so much more to have it all come crashing back down again after working so hard. She felt ruined, contaminated, all over again. She got into bed and curled up in a ball.

Amy followed her and sat down on the bed. It was clear from her face that she was crushed by Lira's reaction. That was why Lira couldn't be mad. She felt bad for Amy, really. She'd been trying so hard, and now she was left to pick up the pieces all over again. She had to be the one, because Lira did not have it in her. She was utterly drained.

Amy reached out and ran her fingers through Lira's hair. "Please, Lira," she begged. "Don't go to that place. Focus on what's around you."

But she couldn't. There was no point in grounding herself in reality anymore, because reality wasn't safe either.

Chapter 25

Lira was still in a bad state the next day, but she was slightly more functional. She agreed to let Amy leave the house and run a few errands, so long as Becky was able to come stay with her. Amy considered leaving her gun with them, but neither woman knew how to fire one and Lira couldn't anyway with her cast, so instead she just brought out an old baseball bat and made sure they both had her and Luis on speed dial.

Amy drove quickly, since she only had until the end of her mother's lunch break. Her first stop was to the jeweler, to pick up Lira's ring. It had been cleaned, polished, and resized, and it looked brand new. Amy couldn't help but stare when she saw it. It *was* a gorgeous ring. It had what the jeweler called an Art Deco design, which would probably make sense to Lira…if she ever got to have the ring. Right now, Amy felt like a complete relationship failure. It was hard to imagine Lira actually *wanting* to marry her.

After that she went to the station to get an update on the case. She had to admit, being back at her desk for a few minutes *did* feel good. She really was itching to get back to work. It made her feel sort of empty to see life going on without her in the Homicide Unit.

"This is the guy I mentioned to you yesterday," Luis said, showing her an old picture. "William Lovett. He went to high school with Nielson, and by all accounts, they had no other friends besides each other. Doesn't mean he's the guy we're looking for, but we'd sure like to talk to him."

"But you can't find him?"

"So far, no."

"How does anybody just disappear in the twenty-first century?" Amy turned away, frustrated, and then turned back. "So how do you get to be one of his victims? Could someone go undercover and lure him in? Because, I'd do it."

Wheeler shook his head. "The way this man hunts is very different from Nielson. He hunts over a wide area, and we don't think he stalks his victims ahead of time. He sees a pretty girl walk away from a crowd, he goes after her. We can't predict where he's going to strike next, or when. There are usually several months between attacks."

"We have to do something," Amy insisted. "Lira found out about him yesterday, and she took it really hard. She stopped eating again. She's barely even talking. The only thing she wants to talk about is our trip to Costa Rica, because she's dying to get out of the damn country, and I don't blame her. At first I thought she was nuts for wanting to run off to the jungle and sleep in a fucking treehouse, but now I can't wait to get there with her. I *cannot* wait. We might just decide to live there from now on."

"How did she find out?" asked Wheeler.

"It was my fault. I was getting messages from Luis, and she could tell something was wrong by how I was acting. Once she asked, I knew I had to tell her because if I didn't, then she'd be freaking out wondering what was so horrible that I couldn't even tell her. I really hoped she'd take it better than she did though. I tried explaining, logically, that there is actually no known threat and that she's already under police protection, but it didn't seem to get through. She's acting like she thinks it's a done deal, that this other serial killer is for sure going to get her, and she *can't* go on like that." She looked from Luis to Wheeler. "You guys, I literally don't think she can take any more. If anything else happens to her right now, it's going to kill her."

"Nothing else is going to happen," promised Wheeler. "She'll feel better once she's on vacation. Get her far away from all of this, give her some fresh air and sunshine, and I bet you'll see the old Lira again."

"I hope so," said Amy. "You have no idea how much I've missed her. I do see glimpses of her, now and then. I know she's still in there."

"So…did you get the ring?" Luis asked her.

Amy broke into a smile in spite of everything. She pulled the ring from her pocket and showed it to Luis and Wheeler. "It was my great-grandmother's ring, from the 1920s."

"It's pretty," said Wheeler. "It might be uncomfortable under her gloves though."

"Don't think I haven't thought of that," said Amy. "I also got her a necklace that's designed to hold a ring, so when she's working, she can put the ring on that and just tuck it in her shirt. That way she still has it with her, but it's not in her way."

"So when are you going to ask her?" Luis inquired.

"I'm not sure yet. I'm going to take the ring with me to Costa Rica, so maybe I can propose in our treehouse, or on the beach, or even on the damn volcano, if that would make her happy." Amy felt nervous about going near an active volcano, but it didn't seem to worry Lira, and apparently it *was* a tourist attraction. "I want to do it when she's happy though. I'm hoping the trip will make her happy, but if it doesn't, then I'll wait until she is. I don't want her associating our engagement with a time when she felt anxious and miserable. And I want to be reasonably confident that she'll say yes."

"Why wouldn't she say yes?"

"I kind of feel like the worst girlfriend in the world right now. I can't find a way to make her feel safe, and I kept a really upsetting secret from her for a month. Now she probably doesn't even trust me anymore."

Wheeler chuckled. "You also allowed yourself to be kidnapped by a serial killer so you could save her, stayed by her side when most people would have run away, and, after surviving something that would destroy most couples, all you want to do is marry her. She's never going to find someone who loves her more than you do."

"No," agreed Amy quietly. "I don't think she will."

***

Amy hurried home so her mom could get back to work. She found Lira sitting on the couch with her computer, Clea at her side and Henry at her feet.

"Hey," said Amy, bending to kiss her girlfriend.

"Hey. How was work?"

"It was good to see everyone. They have a person of interest in the case, but they haven't been able to locate him."

Lira nodded solemnly, looking down at her computer. "I'm planning our itinerary for the trip."

Amy smiled and sat down next to her. "All right, what do you have us doing?"

"Well, there are several different nature hikes I want to go on. I'm planning them all for different days so we don't get too tired. There's also a boat tour that goes through a wildlife refuge. We could have gone canoeing, but I'll have just gotten my cast off, and my wrist will still be weak, so I think the rowing would be too hard for me."

"Yeah, just go for the motor boat," Amy agreed, looking at the website Lira was on. She could see a crocodile (or alligator, whichever it was) in the picture and thought they'd probably be safer on a large boat surrounded by people than in canoes where they could fall into the water and get eaten.

"I also wanted to do a horseback tour, if that's okay with you. It says it's suitable for beginners as well as more experienced riders."

"Sure, why not?"

"And I'd like to visit the wildlife rescue center. And there are several hot springs." She showed Amy a picture of people relaxing in what looked like a pool, but the water was steaming.

"Wow, that looks nice. Can we go to all of them?"

Lira smiled. "We can certainly visit more than one. There's also the hotel spa, which offers massages and mud masks."

"We're doing *all* of that shit. We both have earned the right to have someone pamper the hell out of us."

Lira grinned, and Amy's heart leapt at the sight. "What would you say to a hot air balloon ride?"

Amy bit back the first reply that came to her mind, which was, *What, are you nuts?* Instead she said, "I'll have to think about that one and get back to you."

"It's okay if you don't want to. We have plenty of fun things to do as it is."

"I think we're going to have an *amazing* time."

Lira looked at her carefully. "I'm sorry I got so upset when you told me about that…that man."

Amy touched Lira's hair. "What are you sorry for? I knew it would scare you. That was why I didn't want you to know."

"I am scared, but…I have *you*. I know you won't let anything happen to me."

"Even though I already did?"

"Like you said, this time is different. We know there's a danger. We're prepared."

Amy looked down, hoping she was right. "All the same, I'm glad we'll be getting away for a couple of weeks."

"Me too." She lay her head on Amy's shoulder. "It's impossible not to be nervous, knowing there's someone else out there who might want to hurt me, or hurt *you*. But I'm not going to let it undo all the progress I've made. I have to be stronger than this. I have to be stronger than *him*."

"My sweet girl." Amy wrapped her arms tightly around Lira. "You already are."

Chapter 26

When their plane took off, Lira finally felt like she could breathe again. She watched the Chicago skyline shrinking away below them and reached for Amy's hand—with her right hand, which felt good. She'd gotten her cast off only a few days earlier, and while it would still take about another six weeks to get her strength back in that wrist, it felt good to be unfettered. Now she was going to a place where no one knew anything about what had happened to her, and she no longer had any outward signs of injury for people to ask about. There were still the tally mark scars on her chest, of course, but she had been careful to pack clothes that would cover those.

She was grateful that Amy had been so easy to talk into going on this trip. For all her good qualities, Amy wasn't the most adventurous person, and it wasn't that easy to get her out of Brookwood. But she had agreed to come and had even promised to do whatever activities Lira wanted to do, within reason, as long as she didn't have to explore any caves. Lira had everything all planned out, although she was a little disappointed about the caves.

By the time they got to the hotel, Lira was starting to feel like the past six weeks could have just been a bad dream. She could almost imagine that she and Amy had come straight here the day before her abduction and had left Luis and the others back at home to solve the strange case of the killer who liked to carve tally marks on his victims. And maybe they would find out when they got home that the case had been solved, and there had never been a fourth victim.

The hotel they were staying at had several treehouses, but they were all spread out around a densely-forested area, so you couldn't see one from another. When they climbed the stairs to their own treehouse deck, Lira immediately put her bags down and went to the railing to take in the view. All she could see in any direction were trees, and all she could hear were insects, birds (so many different kinds of birds!), and even the occasional howler monkey. It was so...*alive*, yet peaceful.

"I love it," she breathed.

"Yeah, very isolated," agreed Amy. "If an axe murderer came out of those woods, no one would hear us scream."

Lira gave her a look. "Is there ever a time when you're *not* thinking about homicide?"

"Sorry, old habit." She stepped up behind Lira and put her arms around her waist. "I'm sure there aren't any axe murderers here, and I'm definitely glad we came."

Lira smiled at her. "Really? You're already glad?"

"Absolutely. Even if we had to get back on the plane right now, it would still have been worth coming here just to see the look on your face right now."

Lira smiled brightly and carried her bags inside.

Amy walked around, inspecting their room. There wasn't much there; just a double bed, a small fridge and coffee maker, a tiny closet, an equally tiny bathroom, a desk in the corner, and a shower stall that was out on a private, partially enclosed balcony. The room was small, but there were several large windows in every wall, so it didn't feel cramped. Amy looked interested in the room and its view, but Lira could tell she was also checking to make sure the place was secure, just like she did every night at home. The woman was always on her guard. "What do you want to do first?" she asked Lira when she had completed her inspection.

Lira sat down on the bed and looked up at Amy appraisingly. "You know how you said no one would be able to hear us scream out here?"

"Yes…"

She grinned mischievously. "Wanna test that theory?"

***

Over the next few days, they were much too busy to give a lot of thought to any of their recent problems. Being so active caused Lira to actually work up an appetite and, to Amy's amazement, she ate entire meals without having to force herself. She found herself excitedly chattering to Amy about things they had seen and what they were going to do next, just as she had always done before her life had been shattered.

"This was a perfect day," Lira remarked while she and Amy were sitting out on their little deck one evening, snacking on fresh fruit and watching a mother sloth move along a nearby tree branch with her baby clinging to her. They had spent most of the day hiking through a national park before relaxing in the hot springs. Their hair was still wet, due to the humidity Amy had been complaining about, but it didn't bother Lira. She was really too happy to care.

"I think I know something that would make it even perfect-er," said Amy.

"That's not even a word."

"If Shakespeare could invent words, so can I." She went inside and came back with a bottle of champagne and two glasses.

"Where did you get that?" Lira asked her.

"From our fridge. I actually ordered it this morning, while you were in the shower, so we could have it tonight."

"Why tonight?"

"Why not tonight?"

Lira shrugged and accepted her champagne flute. Amy sat back and sipped, studying Lira fondly. "I really missed you," she said.

"How could you miss me? You've been with me practically 24/7 for the past several weeks."

"I've been with Sad Lira, Scared Lira, Exhausted Lira, sometimes Reasonably Content Lira. And don't get me wrong, I'm crazy about all of them. But I really, really missed Happy Lira. If I'd known she was hiding in Costa Rica, I would have come here a long time ago."

"I'm sorry I've been so—"

"*No*. You have nothing to be sorry for. I'm just really glad to see you smiling again! I forgot how beautiful you are when you're happy. Of course you're always gorgeous, but...Happy Lira kinda glows."

"I think I overreacted, when you told me about the other unsub." It was the first time either of them had explicitly mentioned the troubles they'd left behind, and Lira felt like she might be breaking an unwritten code, but she didn't know whether she would still be thinking this clearly when they got back home.

"I wouldn't say you overreacted. I think you have every right to be scared, I mean I'm scared too. I don't want anything to happen to either of us. But I don't like to see you totally consumed by fear. Then it's like he got you without even getting you."

Lira nodded. "I know. I'll try to be better, when we get back. We need to *live* again."

"Does that mean I get to take Happy Lira back to Brookwood with me?"

Lira smiled. "I'll try really hard to get her on the plane. But I'm sure the others will be there too."

"That's fine, as long as I can see you smile sometimes. Like really smile, not just to be polite." Amy poured more champagne. "But to tell you the truth, you've handled the whole situation so much better than I would have if I'd been the one taken. I had a hard enough time just with what Flynn did; if I'd gone through what you went through, I'd probably still be curled up in a ball crying all day. And I would definitely have pushed you away, because I would be afraid you'd see me differently. I wouldn't get therapy except for whatever the department forced me to do. I would have just let myself fall apart. But you, you're amazing. You're so much braver than I am."

"I think maybe we're each a different kind of brave. You do a lot of brave things I don't think I could do." She frowned. "But please don't ever pull away from me if something bad happens to you. I couldn't handle that."

"I won't. I know better now." Amy took Lira's hand and squeezed it. "I have something really important to ask you, but I'm not sure how."

Lira's stomach clenched. "Why aren't you sure how? Is it something upsetting?"

Amy smiled. "No, not at all. It's just kind of big."

Lira met her eyes uncertainly. "So just say it."

"I...well, I just...maybe I should wait until later."

"No," said Lira, tilting her head thoughtfully. "I think you should finish what you started. Ask me the question."

Amy bit her lip. "Well, I'm doing it wrong." She got up and knelt down in front of Lira, taking her hand. Lira drew in her breath.

"Lira Jade Ward," began Amy. She seemed too nervous to meet Lira's eyes and was staring absently at her breasts instead. "I...I love you. I love everything about you. I love you more than anything. And I would really, really like it if you would be my — shit, I forgot something!" She started to stand up, but Lira pushed her back down.

"Finish asking the question and then you can get whatever you forgot," Lira told her sharply.

"But the thing I forgot is part of the question."

"I said *finish*."

Amy looked at her helplessly and let out her breath. "I was wondering if you would marry me?"

Lira smiled slowly. "That must have been the worst proposal ever."

"I'm *sorry!* I didn't really rehearse it. Do you want me to try again a different night?"

"No. It was also the best." She put her arms around Amy's neck and kissed her. "Do you want all the Liras, or just the happy one?"

"All of them. The entire package deal. But if you accept, you have to put up with all the Amys."

"I can do that." She kissed her again. "I would love to marry you."

"Really?" Relief washed over Amy's face. "I was so worried you would say no. There's a ring too!" She dashed inside and came out a minute later carrying a tiny box. "I don't know if you'll like it. It belonged to my mother's mother's mother, when she was engaged, way back in the Roaring Twenties. My mom wanted me to give it to you."

Lira put her hand on her chest, touched. "Your mother wanted *me* to have a family heirloom ring?"

"Are you kidding me? She's already calling you her

daughter-in-law."

Tears welled up in Lira's eyes. "That's so sweet of her. I'm sure I'll love the ring."

Amy cracked open the box and showed it to her. It was silver, with a big emerald surrounded by tiny rose-cut diamonds in an intricate design. It was perfect.

"Put it on me," Lira requested, holding out her hand. Amy carefully removed the ring from its box and slid it onto Lira's finger.

"There, it's official now," Amy announced.

Lira's tears spilled over. She threw her arms around Amy.

"These are happy tears, right?" Amy asked her.

"Yes! I'm happy that you still want to marry me after everything we've been through!"

"Still? Actually, I want to more than ever." She pulled back and looked at Lira. "Like you said when you wanted me to move in with you, life is too short to put things off. And it's not like I'm ever going to find anyone else who's even half as incredible, or as adorable, as you."

Lira grinned. "I certainly hope not!"

"So, you wanna go in and have really hot celebratory sex?"

Lira's eyes widened. It was the first time Amy had actually brought up sex on her own since the kidnapping, and it made Lira happier than she could say. "I would *love* that," she said.

Amy took Lira's hand and led her inside the treehouse, carefully locking the door behind them. Lira got in bed and looked at Amy expectantly. She knew Amy had been on eggshells recently, so frightened of accidentally triggering her that Lira had to basically outline what she wanted Amy to do to her every time, and Lira was ready to be done with that. She wanted things to be more equal again.

Amy, perhaps getting the memo, got into bed and pulled Lira's shirt off without further prompting. Lira eagerly yanked off Amy's tank top and bra as well.

"We have to decide on a wedding venue," Lira announced, teasing Amy's nipples.

Amy gently cupped Lira's breasts. "Well, yeah, I guess so."

She bent down and ran her tongue over each breast.

"I've always wanted an outdoor wedding, in a garden setting. Would you be interested in something like that?"

"Yeah, sure. We can research venues when we get home. I'm kinda busy right now." Amy began working her way downwards, brushing her fingers lightly over Lira's skin to give her goosebumps. She eased off Lira's pants and ran her fingers back and forth along the inside of her thigh, stopping just short of her heat each time.

"Amy," Lira murmured. "Just touch me."

"Touch you where?" Amy asked innocently.

"You *know* where." She would have told her explicitly, but Amy hated it when she used technical terms in bed, and Lira preferred to call things by their real names.

Amy, no doubt hoping to continue avoiding the use of proper medical terms for the female anatomy during sex, obediently slid her fingers back down Lira's thigh, onto her vulva, and began caressing her outer and then inner labia.

"Mmmm," moaned Lira blissfully. "I think I'm going to ask Clarissa to be my maid of honor. She's become a really good friend."

"Indeed she has, but she doesn't belong in bed with us," Amy replied. She took Lira's left nipple in her mouth while stroking her clit slowly with two fingers. Lira wrapped her arms around Amy, holding her in place as she pressed harder on her clit and slid her free hand up to cup Lira's right breast. Lira came loudly, her back arched, hands clutching at Amy's hair.

Amy maintained pressure for a moment longer before stretching out beside Lira. Lira rolled onto her side and reached for Amy, caressing the familiar contours of her body.

"The Willis Mansion hosts weddings," she remarked. "They have a lovely garden, and a ballroom for receptions."

"Great. Let's do that."

"*Amy.* You're just agreeing to everything I say."

"Because right now my biggest concern is whether you're going to fuck me or not."

Lira broke into a grin. She watched Amy's face as she slid one, and then two, fingers inside of her, curling them to stimulate the spongy area she knew so well. With her left hand she reached for Amy's hand and placed it between her own legs. "You do me too," she whispered, and Amy eagerly slid her long fingers inside of Lira, matching her stroke for stroke. Lira came first, and, feeling it was unfair, quickly focused her full attention on Amy. She nudged Amy onto her back, knelt between her legs and, applying full pressure to her G-spot with her fingers, sucked Amy's clit into her mouth.

I will get to taste her like this, make love to her like this, for the rest of my life, Lira thought, feeling as though her heart might explode. She moved her tongue and fingers in sync until Amy screamed out her orgasm, no doubt frightening the nearby wildlife. Lira started to withdraw, but Amy seized her head and pulled her closer, so Lira resumed what she was doing until she felt Amy riding the crest of another glorious orgasm.

Feeling quite pleased with herself, Lira slid her body on top of Amy's in one fluid motion, gazing down into Amy's eyes. "I really, really love you," she breathed.

"I know." Amy touched Lira's face. "You're kind of my favorite thing ever."

Lira beamed. "You're kind of *my* favorite thing ever, too." She kissed Amy and shifted her weight, pressing her wet, swollen pussy against Amy's. She began moving her hips, rubbing her clit against Amy's gently, and then harder, until they strained together with almost simultaneous orgasms.

Afterwards they lay facing each other, legs intertwined, listening to the birds sing outside. Lira wondered if Amy was thinking the same thing she was: that this was a lot like the night before the abduction, that they were finally getting back to that place. She raised her left hand and examined her ring again. She wasn't sure what her mother would say when she told her, but she realized she didn't care as much as she used to. She had a new family now that loved her exactly the way she was.

"Did you ever think you'd be marrying a woman?" Amy

asked her suddenly.

"No," Lira admitted. "But then, I didn't really expect to get married. I liked fantasizing about what my wedding would be like if I had one, but I didn't really want a husband that much, so..."

"Mm. Well, now you get the wedding without the husband. How cool is that?"

Lira grinned at her. "Very cool. Before we were together as a couple, I always hoped you'd never get married either, because I wanted to still be your first priority. I knew it was selfish, but I hoped it anyway."

"You could never stop being my first priority," Amy said softly. "Besides, you know I never would have married some guy."

Lira took Amy's hand and slowly ran her thumb over each finger. "So what made you want to marry me?"

"Well, you're *you*."

Lira laughed. "You're going to have to be more specific than that."

Amy thought it over. "I kind of figured when we got together that it was going to end up being a lifelong thing. I mean, as important as you were to me, I wouldn't have tried to change the nature of our relationship unless I believed we could make it last. And then when I moved in with you, same thing. I wouldn't have done it unless I felt like it was going to be permanent. So I guess it was always in the back of my mind that we would probably get married eventually. It just made sense. But then recent events made me feel like we should do it sooner rather than later."

"How so?"

"Well..." Amy put an arm over Lira, somewhat protectively. "When you were gone, all I could think about was how I couldn't live without you, how my life would be over if I didn't get you back. You had become like the center of my universe, you know? I didn't have any kind of plan for how to go on without you. I just knew I couldn't do it. And I was also worried, if we did find you alive, about what sort of state you'd be in. We had nothing to go on. I was afraid of weeks or months passing, and you going through that torture the whole time... so I was afraid of the psychological damage you might have when we found you. It's like soldiers who've been in combat; sometimes they're never the same again. If you'd been there two or three months, it was possible that the damage would have been irreversible. You could have had such a severe case of PTSD that you'd never function normally again. I was trying to brace myself for the fact that even if I got you back, you might not be the same person I lost, and all I could think about was how to take care of you if that happened. I was worried about not being good enough, but it never crossed my mind to give up on you. I would have stayed, if you let me, and looked after you forever no matter what condition you were in." Her voice broke and she swallowed. "And when you feel that strongly about someone, it doesn't make any sense *not* to marry her."

Lira wiped a tear away. "I would do the same for you," she said softly. "Take care of you, I mean. Even if you weren't the same anymore."

Amy pulled Lira closer. "I know."

"And you thought I'd say no." Lira started giggling.

"I didn't know what you'd say! I was *afraid* you'd say no."

"You are going to look so beautiful in your dress."

"I *knew* you were going to say that. That much I did know, that if you accepted, you were going to put me in a wedding dress."

"Well, you picked the wrong bride if you want to get married in jeans and a t-shirt."

"I know, I know."

Lira closed her eyes happily, envisioning wedding dresses and flowers and cake and champagne. She knew her dreams would not take her to any dark places that night.

Chapter 27

Amy walked out of the police station and headed for the morgue. She and Lira had been back at work for a few weeks now, and Amy was relishing every moment of having their old routine back. She loved solving murders with Luis. She loved knowing none of the dead bodies were going to have tally marks on them. And, most of all, she loved being able to go next door and see Lira in the morgue, doing what she was best at.

Lira had been amazing since coming back. Amy knew the autopsies had to be a little more unsettling for her now, but she wasn't letting it get in the way of her doing her job. There had only been one real hiccup so far, when Lira had to do her first rape kit after returning. Amy had wanted her to turn that autopsy over to someone else, but Lira refused, and she got all the way through collecting and labelling semen samples before breaking down and locking herself in her office. But she even handled that situation admirably, calling Amy over to comfort her for a while before going back to finish the autopsy.

Amy was also very impressed with how well Lira was doing outside of work. She was now seeing her therapist only once a week and had, to the best of her ability, kept her promise not to live in fear of the unsub Nielson had been communicating with. It helped that Amy had given her a distraction in the form of wedding planning. *That* was taking up an enormous amount of time. As Amy had predicted, her mother and Lira were going nuts with wedding ideas, sometimes scheming together and sometimes butting heads. What she had not predicted was that they wanted *her* to have an opinion on *everything*. Amy really didn't have opinions about flower arrangements, color schemes, or music selections, but she quickly learned that "I don't care, do whatever you want" was *always* the wrong answer.

As for Amy, the time had come to accept that she needed to find a therapist of her own. It was happening more and more often for her now: the nightmares about Lira vanishing and never coming home, the overwhelming fear of someone else hurting Lira, the intrusive thoughts that took her completely out of the present moment. It was like she had been unconsciously waiting for Lira to get better so she could fall apart herself. A certain rage had been building up in her ever since Lira was taken. She was outraged that Lira had become one of Nielson's victims. She felt like some sacred law had been broken, which she supposed was how the loved ones of every victim of violent crime felt, but still. This was *Lira*. Nothing like that was ever supposed to happen to her. Even though Lira was now getting her life back and generally handling the situation like a motherfucking boss, Amy could not stop wishing for a way to undo everything that had happened. She hated that Lira had to go through that, she hated knowing that it would affect her in some way or another throughout her life, and she *hated* that Lira was currently looking at wedding dresses and ruling out a lot of the ones she liked because they were too low-cut and would show her tally mark scars. She knew the rage would tear her apart eventually if she didn't do something about it.

Amy walked into Lira's office and found her huddled by the computer with Clarissa, looking way too happy to be working on an autopsy report.

"Are you looking at wedding dresses again?" Amy asked.

Lira looked up and smiled. "I was just showing Clarissa some of my favorites while I waited for you to get here."

"Mm hm. So, do you think you're going to get it narrowed down before the wedding?"

"I am narrowing it down right now. I'll be ready to work on yours as soon as I've settled on mine."

"Well, you'll look gorgeous in whatever you choose. You could come down the aisle in your lab coat and I wouldn't complain."

"Amy, I'm only planning to get married once. It needs to be perfect, for both of us."

It already is, thought Amy, but she didn't like to get mushy in front of Clarissa. "So, about this dead body?"

"Oh yes!" Lira led her to the refrigerated storage room, pulling out the body she wanted to discuss. Amy could see that Lira had her ring on the chain she had gotten her. She kept fondling it absent-mindedly, which made Amy smile. "So, his injuries are consistent with being hit by a car, but I don't think he was hit in the neighborhood you found him in. There are chunks of gravel embedded in his head. See?"

"Gross," said Amy. "But there was no gravel in the area we found him in."

"Exactly. So they must have transported the body after they hit him."

"So instead of a hit and run, it's more of a hit, load body into car, dump body somewhere else, and run?"

"I think so."

"So, if it was a gravel road, that means it was outside of Brookwood. Someplace rural."

"Or in someone's driveway."

"Well wherever it was, they had a reason for not wanting to leave the body there. Do you think you could find out where he was hit from the gravel?"

"Possibly. I already took samples. It's pea gravel, which means he was probably hit in a driveway. If we could find all the driveways that have this exact type and color of gravel, then we could search them all for signs of blood, and match it to the victim. It might be a lot of driveways, though…" She looked up and eyed Amy carefully. "I've been looking at A-line and ball gowns for myself, but I think a sheath would be more suited to your body type."

"Mm. So this is being ruled a homicide, right?"

"Yes!"

"Just checking."

Lira zipped the body bag back up and led Amy back to her office.

"Are you all set for your mom's arrival tonight?" Amy asked her. Lira had avoided her mother's calls for the first several weeks after her kidnapping, but after returning from Costa Rica, she had called to tell her mother about the engagement. Her mother had made another offer to visit, which Lira took her up on this time.

"Yes, I think so. I've decided I'm not going to worry about making everything perfect. She has to accept my life as is. I can't alter it to please her."

"I think that's a good way of looking at it."

"I invited your mother to dinner. I thought our moms should meet, since we're getting married."

"Should be interesting. You think your mom's okay with you marrying a cop?"

"I don't think she'll ever complain about me marrying *you*."

"Why not?"

Lira looked up and smiled. "She knows you saved me."

***

Amy went with Lira to pick Genevieve Ward up from the airport. She could tell her fiancée was nervous, but also excited. She had wanted this for a long time. As for Amy, she would be watching like a hawk to make sure Genevieve treated Lira the way she deserved to be treated, because she damn well wasn't going to put up with anything less.

Lira hung back uncertainly as Genevieve strolled through the arrivals gate, head held high, well-dressed as usual. But then she lit up at the sight of her daughter and held her arms out, and Lira became a little girl again, running eagerly to her mother's arms. Genevieve held her close, murmuring, "Oh, my sweet Lira, I've missed you so much." Amy searched the older woman's face for some resemblance to the woman she loved, but found nothing. Genevieve's eyes were brown, and her hair had been brown once, although it was mostly gray now. Amy thought perhaps she saw a trace of Lira in her jawline, but she wasn't sure. Lira's looks didn't come from this woman, but her mannerisms certainly did. She could see that when Lira stepped back and the two exchanged pleasantries for a moment.

"And Amy," said Genevieve, turning, "I hear you are to be my daughter-in-law, so you'd better hug me as well."

"Oh," said Amy in surprise. "Um, okay." She stepped forward and awkwardly hugged the woman who would be her mother-in-law a year from now, although she hadn't yet thought about it in those terms.

"I'm looking forward to getting to know you better," Genevieve told her. "The way Lira gushes about you, I am certain I will come to love you just as much as she does."

"Okay, well maybe not *quite* as much," said Amy uncertainly. Lira just laughed.

***

Amy was relieved at how well dinner went with the two moms. Genevieve had no interest in taking part in the wedding planning, but she did volunteer to pick up the tabs so her only child could have exactly the wedding she wanted. Amy knew it would be polite to at least try to turn down the money, but she couldn't bring herself to do it. She wanted Lira to have her dream wedding too, and she didn't quite have the funds to give it to her. Genevieve did.

After Becky left, Lira gave Genevieve a formal tour of the house, and then they all settled in the living room with a bottle of wine and the engagement present Genevieve had brought: an album she'd put together of Lira's childhood photos. Lira hadn't seen many of the pictures in years and was quite excited about them; Amy hadn't seen them at all and rather enjoyed the shots of Little Lira travelling the world with her mother. Their closeness was quite evident in the pictures.

"Look!" said Amy. "It's you in front of Big Ben!"

"Well," said Lira, "I was in front of the clock tower at the Palace of Westminster."

"Isn't the clock tower named Big Ben?"

"No, the main bell is named Big Ben."

"Why does the *bell* have a name? Every time I've seen a picture of that clock, people have called it Big Ben."

"It's a common misconception."

"That was the year we lived in London, when Lira was eight," said Genevieve fondly. "By the end of the year she was speaking with a full British accent. It was adorable!"

"Oh, I wanna hear you talk with that accent," said Amy with a grin.

Lira blushed. "I can't do it anymore."

"That's where she learned her love of tea," continued Genevieve. "Our housekeeper would make her a cup of tea every day when she got home from school. She got in the habit and kept asking for it even after we came back to the States. I always had to keep some in the house."

"So *that's* why you're like that," said Amy, draining the last of her wine. "Well, that's the end of this bottle. Should I open another one?"

"Why not? It's a special occasion!" said Genevieve. "I'll come help you."

Lira continued to page through the album while Amy and Genevieve went into the kitchen.

"It's so wonderful to spend time with her again," said Genevieve, carefully selecting another bottle of wine.

"I'm sure it is." Amy got out the corkscrew. "It makes me wonder, though, why you've pushed her away so much of her adult life."

Genevieve took the corkscrew from Amy and focused intently on the task of opening the wine bottle. "As you might have seen from those pictures, Lira was my world. I suppose it stung a bit when she reached adulthood and made it clear she wanted her own world, one that did not have me in it."

"She just wanted her independence, like any healthy adult. The way she explained it, it sounds like you didn't approve of her career choice."

"Well, who wants to think of their daughter spending her days dissecting dead people?"

"If she was going to look for her father by testing her DNA, she'd have done it by now."

Genevieve's head snapped up. "I never said that was my concern."

"No, but it's the only thing that makes sense. I know you've never wanted to talk to her about her father, and she tries to believe you have a good reason, but I just need to know: are you protecting her, or protecting him?"

"I'm protecting *her*. I have no need or desire to protect him."

"So you know who he is?"

She hesitated. "Yes."

"Do you understand the impact not knowing has had on her? It's been damaging to her self-esteem having her origins shrouded in secrecy her whole life. She doesn't know where half of her came from, and it makes her feel like she has something to be ashamed of. Would knowing the truth really hurt her more than this?"

"Yes," said Genevieve, this time with no hesitation. "It would hurt her very much to know."

"So he's not a good person."

"No, he's not, and you have no idea what you'd be uncovering if you tried to find him. Please. I know you love her. Just please, leave it alone. She's been through enough as it is."

Amy considered this. "Does he know about Lira?"

Genevieve gave her an arresting look. "No," she said thoughtfully. "He doesn't know about Lira."

"Then why did you move so much? Was he after *you*?"

Genevieve was quiet for some time, examining her fingers. "He had no reason to come after me," she said quietly. "But if he'd found out about Lira – that she was his – I am certain he would have come after her, and she would have been in great danger. That was what I lived in fear of. It's something I still fear, but it doesn't look like I can protect her anymore."

"You could have warned her, at least, that you believed him to be dangerous, so she wouldn't try to find him."

"Would she have listened? Will you?"

Amy considered that. "For now, it's enough for me to know that she's safer this way. I'm not going to stir anything up that could upset her, or endanger her, when she's still healing from her attack. But I think she deserves to know the whole story someday, however painful it may be."

Genevieve nodded. "That's fair enough. Just promise me it won't be soon."

"I think it's up to you and her to decide when the whole

story should come out."

An expression of relief and gratitude washed over Genevieve's features, but suddenly their conversation was interrupted by a piercing scream from the living room. They both raced into the room to find a trembling Lira.

"I saw a man looking in the window, from the porch!" she told them.

"What did he look like?" Amy demanded, peering into the darkness and trying to recall the picture she'd seen of William Lovett.

"I couldn't tell. I just saw his silhouette, but someone was definitely there!"

Fuck. They no longer had an officer stationed on their street. The department had decided they couldn't keep using resources for that when no actual threat had been made.

"Okay," said Amy resolutely. "I'll get my gun."

"No, Amy, just call for help! I don't want you to go out there!"

"You call for help," Amy told her. "I'm gonna make sure the bastard doesn't get away."

She took her gun and a flashlight, just like the night she'd heard a possum outside, but she knew in her gut it wasn't going to go down the same way this time. She went out the front door, doing her best to keep her back to the wall as she shined her light around the porch. No one there. She stepped down slowly and began to look around the driveway. Suddenly she felt cold steel against her throat.

"Drop the gun," said a low voice in her ear.

Amy froze, considering her options. If she made a sudden move, she might be able to take him off guard, get the upper hand.

Or he might kill her, and Lira would be devastated.

Backup would be on the way, she reminded herself. Anything she did now was temporary. She put down the gun.

"Good girl," he said, taking her arm with his left hand and pushing her in front of him. "Now I want you to come with me nice and quiet."

"And if I don't? "

"I kill you and take your girlfriend. It's all the same to me."

"So you must be William Lovell."

"And I already know you're Amy Sadler. You killed the only person who ever understood me. I'm going to finish what he started."

"I have backup on the way, you know."

"And we'll be gone by the time they get here. Let's go."

He urged her towards the street, and she didn't see what choice she had but to go. She stepped towards the waiting truck, trying to calculate how she could slow him down without getting hurt too badly, when she heard a loud crack behind her. The hand that was gripping her fell away, and the knife at her throat clattered to the ground.

She turned around to see Lira standing behind them, Amy's old baseball bat in her hands.

Chapter 28

The man was lying on the ground, gripping his head in pain, which meant he was still conscious. He could still try to hurt them.

Lira wasn't sure what to do. Should she hit him again? She'd never intentionally hurt someone before, but she felt like she'd come out of her own head when she saw that he had her Amy. She held the bat at the ready while Amy grabbed the fallen knife. The bat suddenly felt heavy and wrong in her hands, but she continued gripping it tightly. She would do what she had to.

"Hey sweetie, let's get you away from here," said Amy gently, taking Lira's arm and steering her back to the front yard.

"He's still conscious," Lira told her. "He could still—"

"He won't. I just have to grab my gun." Amy ran up the driveway, and Lira realized her mother had followed her outside.

"Are you okay?" Genevieve asked, her hand on Lira's arm. "What happened?"

Lira shook her head, unable to answer just yet. Her eyes were on the man in the street, who was pushing himself into a sitting position. Lira wrenched herself away from her mother, raising the bat once more.

"Not so fast." Amy emerged from the shadows, her gun leveled at the man on the street. She walked right up to him fearlessly.

"For fuck's sake, you threaten a man while he's down?" He patted around on the ground.

"Whereas the women you raped and killed were in perfect fighting condition. Put your hands up. Your knife's not down there."

He put his hands up, raising his eyes to Amy. "Who the hell hit me?"

"That would be my lovely fiancée, the last woman your pal Nielson planned to kill."

His eyes moved to Lira and then back to Amy. "You know I could do more for you in one night than she ever has."

"And then you'd kill me."

"I'd give you the best night of your life first."

"Please," Amy scoffed. "You're not even worth her spit."

Lira could hear sirens in the distance, and she relaxed just a tiny bit, knowing Luis would be here soon to arrest the man and then Amy would be safe, and so would she.

Suddenly he lunged at Amy, making a desperate grab for her gun. Without thinking, Lira started to run towards them, her mind consumed with fear for Amy's safety. But Amy was faster, quickly firing off two shots: one low shot that made him crumple to the ground, and another to the head that meant he wouldn't be getting back up. Lira froze in her tracks, stunned by the noise. She had never heard a gunshot before, and her ears were now ringing so badly that she could no longer hear the approaching sirens, but she did see Luis's car pull up.

And then Amy was at her side again, her lips moving as she reached to take the bat from Lira. Lira couldn't understand her, so she just relinquished the bat and wrapped her arms around her fiancée, who held her close. Lira clutched her and felt tears coming, although she wasn't sure what she was crying about.

"Is everyone okay?" said Luis's voice beside them, and Lira realized her hearing was starting to come back.

"Yeah, we're okay," said Amy. "We finally found William Lovett, and Lira decided it was time to show the world she's a fucking badass."

Luis looked at the body in the street. "*She* did this?"

"Well, I'm the one who shot him," said Amy. "But I couldn't have done it if Lira hadn't taken him down with my baseball bat first." She gave Lira an admiring smile.

Lira smiled back uncertainly. "I couldn't let him hurt you the way he hurt me…I mean, the way his friend hurt me. I didn't want you to suffer like that." She hugged Amy tighter, the tears still flowing down her face. "I couldn't let him take you away from me."

Amy kissed her cheek. "And you didn't."

***

There was a knock at the door the following day while Amy

was having lunch with Lira and Genevieve. None of them had been able to sleep much the night before, and Lira had postponed their plans to try on wedding dresses, but they were trying to have a normal day aside from that. Amy got up to answer the door and found Luis on the front porch, grinning happily.

"You'll never guess where I just came from," he said.

"Where?"

"William Lovett's apartment."

"No shit! How'd you find it?" Amy glanced behind her to see that Lira had come into the room.

"We found some old mail when we searched his truck and went to check out the address. I know it'll be a few weeks before we get final confirmation from the DNA results, but I think we found enough to say definitively that this is our other killer, the one Nielson was collecting articles about."

Lira let out her breath. "So it's over? There's no one left to come after us?"

"It's over," Luis told her gently. "There's no evidence that he or Nielson were palling around with any other creeps." He looked at Amy like he wanted to say more, but didn't think he should in front of Lira.

"Oh Amy." Lira turned to her fiancée and hugged her. "I was so worried we would still be dealing with this at our wedding! Do you realize what this means?" She stepped back. "We don't have to look over our shoulders anymore. We can just...*live*."

Amy smiled at her. "We sure can." She turned back to Luis. "What else did you want to say?"

He looked at her uncertainly. "It's not much, it's just that, it's clear he was still actively communicating with Nielson. He had pictures that Nielson must have sent him of all his victims, like the ones he sent us, with tally marks on the back. It was the same pattern he followed with us, except that there was an early picture of the first victim, Kelly Bruin, as well."

"So he would send a picture when he first took someone, and again after he killed her?"

"Yes, and sometimes a few in between as well. He definitely

wanted to keep Lovett up to speed."

"Was there one of me?" Lira asked softly.

Luis nodded gravely. "Just one, like the one he sent us. So Lovett did know about you all along. He was probably just waiting for the right time to strike, when there wouldn't be a patrol car outside anymore."

Lira seemed to be turning that over in her mind. Amy put an arm around her. "I wouldn't have let him touch you though, and thanks to you, he didn't hurt me either."

"Word's getting around that you took down a serial killer," Luis said, smiling at Lira. "Nobody wants to get on your bad side now! You're just as dangerous as your fiancée."

"I always knew she had it in her," said Amy proudly.

"But seriously, you two are in the clear now. You can just focus on getting married. I'm looking forward to that wedding!" He winked at Amy. "I told you, didn't I?"

Amy laughed and shook her head as he left, then turned back to Lira. "We've been a couple, what, almost nine months now?"

Lira nodded.

"You realize that our entire relationship, we've been dealing with this tally marks guy and then his friend. And now we're finally done with both of them."

Lira smiled sadly. "As much as we can be, anyway."

"We can be, and we *are*. It's over. They're both dead. There won't be any more victims from either of them."

"Except one victim lived." Lira held Amy's gaze, unblinking. "And I'm always going to have the marks. You'll always have to see them, and be reminded."

"You're not a victim anymore. You're a survivor now." Amy felt the familiar rage rising in her and fought it, as she always did around Lira, for fear that Lira would think it was directed at her. She had actually researched scar removal online, unbeknownst to Lira, but every article she found said that surgery could only reduce the appearance of scars; it couldn't erase them entirely, which Lira undoubtedly knew already. "Anyway, your scars don't have to remind us of the case. To me they're a reminder that you're still here, which means we won, which means it's *over*."

"Well, it *has* been nearly three months, so it's possible I would be dead by now, if things had gone according to plan." Amy had noticed that Lira never said Nielson's name. She'd heard it plenty of times, so she had to know what it was, but for whatever reason, she never spoke it.

"But, you're alive, and planning a *wedding*," Amy said, eager to get Lira's mind back on happier topics. "And I love you more than ever."

Lira smiled. "I love you more than ever too."

"I hate to interrupt," said Genevieve, cautiously stepping into the foyer, "but are you two planning on finishing lunch?"

"Of course!" said Amy, taking Lira's hand and walking back to the dining room. "I trust you overheard our conversation with my partner?"

"I heard enough. So it's been confirmed that you two ladies are no longer in any danger?"

"That is correct," said Lira, sitting down at the table.

"So," Genevieve said with a smile, "does that mean we're back on for dress shopping this afternoon?"

Lira broke into a grin. "Most definitely!"

Epilogue

Lira stood by the window of the third-floor ballroom in the Willis Mansion and looked out at the empty garden, where just a few hours earlier she and Amy had taken their vows. It had gotten dark out, but there were strategically placed lights throughout the beautifully landscaped yard, which gave it a sort of haunting look. It was the first moment during the reception that Lira had found herself standing alone, and she doubted it would last long, but she was grateful to have a chance to catch her breath. She wasn't even sure where Amy was, but she knew she had to turn up sooner or later.

She fingered her new ring, a silver band engraved with a leaf pattern, just like Amy's. With this ring came not only a new life, but a new name, at least in her personal life. Professionally she would still be known as Dr. Lira Ward, but outside of work she was going to start using the name Sadler. Lira was proud of being an official part of the Sadler family now, of having an entire family to call her own, and she wanted to brag about it.

It had been easy telling Amy she would always be there for her, that she would hold her and cherish her for the rest of her life no matter what happened. The words would have been true even if she hadn't said them aloud. She wasn't forsaking anything for Amy, because Amy was all she wanted anyway. They had already been through so much together that all the promises they had to make just seemed like a formality. Still, hearing Amy actually say it – being reminded that this amazing person genuinely wanted to spend the rest of her life with *her* – had felt almost unreal. Amy had looked her straight in the eyes as she said every word, her voice breaking with emotion a few times. She really meant it, that Lira was the person she loved most, that she wanted only her forever.

They had agreed in advance that each of them would engrave something on the inside of the other's ring, but that neither would know what her own ring said until the ceremony. Lira had waited in anticipation as Luis handed her ring to Amy, who then held it up to Lira and began to speak.

"When I got you this ring, I had trouble figuring out what to put on the inside," she told Lira, speaking just barely loud enough for everyone to hear. "How could I possibly explain why I love you in such a small space? And then I realized that was a stupid question. I can easily sum up what I love about you in just one word: *everything*. I love *everything* about you. I say it all the time, and I know you don't always believe me, but it's true. I love your big brain and your even bigger heart and every weird little quirk." Lira laughed, and Amy continued. "So I put that one word inside your ring, so you can have it against your skin for the rest of your life and remember that, no matter how the rest of the world might treat you, *I* love every tiny little thing about you. And I always will." She took Lira's left hand and slid the ring onto her finger.

And just like that, Lira was Amy's. Officially. Permanently.

"I had trouble deciding what to put on yours as well," Lira said, holding up Amy's ring. "And what I did put will probably seem very unoriginal to a lot of people. You are many things to me, but in your ring I simply put, 'my hero,' because you are, in every sense of the term. Not only have you saved me from harm more than once, but you've saved me from the life I would have lived if you weren't in it, the life I *was* living before I met you. It wasn't a miserable life, but it was hardly an ecstatic one, and that is how you make me feel every day: ecstatic. You have brought so much unimaginable joy into my life. You're also the bravest, most caring person I know. I know you don't think of yourself as a hero, but I hope you can accept this lifelong reminder that I consider you to be mine." She took Amy's hand then, blinking back tears as she did so, and slid the ring onto Amy's finger.

And just like that, Amy was hers. Officially. Permanently.

Lira had felt a single tear slip down her face before she kissed Amy, and when they turned to walk back up the aisle, she saw her mother openly weeping in the front row.

She was glad that her relationship with her mother was in a better place now. Having Genevieve there to help her get ready for the wedding, to walk her down the aisle and watch her commit herself to the love of her life, meant the world to her. She still didn't feel like their relationship was quite what it had once been, and she wasn't sure it ever would be until her mother decided to be more open with her about the past, but at least for today she was happy with the way things were. Her mother was there with all her support, fully accepting Amy as her daughter-in-law. That was more than enough for now.

And then there was Becky, who was practically running the reception. Lira knew this scenario wasn't exactly what she'd always dreamed of for Amy, but in the end all she cared about was seeing her daughter happy. Lira could not possibly have asked for a better mother-in-law, or for better siblings-in-law than Amy's sister and brother. Nor could she have asked for better coworkers and friends than Clarissa, Luis, and Wheeler. Clarissa had now finished her residency and had been hired full-time as a forensic pathologist in the Geneva County Coroner's Office, which meant she would be working alongside Lira for a long time to come, and she was overjoyed to be Lira's maid of honor. Luis had stood up with Amy during the wedding, which meant a lot to all of them since this day might not have happened without his help.

It had been over a year since Lira's abduction and rape. In her mind she tended to think of it simply as the event that had shattered her entire life, at a time when life was better than it had ever been before. She wasn't so bitter about that now. It had taken time, but she had put her life back together, and now it was even better than before the abduction. What happened could easily have torn her and Amy apart, but somehow, it had brought them closer together instead. And because of that, Lira really had no fear for the future of their relationship, their marriage. She was pretty sure they could handle anything by now.

She had come a long way since it happened. While at first she had felt completely destroyed, now most of the time she felt like some sort of mighty warrior for having gotten through it. She still had her bad days, of course. There were certain things that could trigger her and throw her off for an entire day, sometimes longer, but it was happening less often as time went on. She still saw her therapist every other week, and that helped. Amy had even put in almost a year with her own therapist to help her deal with what happened, which made Lira proud. She knew Amy wasn't the biggest fan of sitting around talking about her feelings.

Oddly, she found that she no longer remembered certain things about her attacker, while other details were still much too clear. She couldn't remember his face at all, and she had a really hard time remembering his name, even though she'd heard Amy and the others mention it several times. But she remembered the feel of his hands on her so clearly some days that she wanted to climb right out of her skin, and for some reason, she remembered the sound of his breathing. That remained her biggest trigger: if she heard someone in public whose breathing reminded her of his, she had to leave immediately. Fortunately, it was not a common occurrence, and Amy was very understanding. Lira felt like she had fallen in love with Amy in a whole new way through this otherwise very negative experience.

"Hey." Lira looked around and saw Amy coming up behind her, looking stunning in her lace sheath dress, her hair swept up with just a few curls hanging down by her face. "It's a nice view, isn't it?"

Lira smiled. "I like this view better," she said, tracing Amy's form with her eyes. "I know I said it already, but you look gorgeous in that dress."

"And I'm glad you like it, but I won't pretend I'm not looking forward to taking it back off."

Lira tilted her head, unable to suppress a devious grin. "Well, I won't pretend I'm not looking forward to taking it off you."

Amy chuckled, wrapping her arms around Lira's waist. "We could just go."

"We can't leave early! It's *our* party!"

"Yes, it is *our* party, which means no one can stop us from leaving. Come on, there's only an hour left anyway. Let's go break in our marriage bed."

Lira frowned. "But we still have the same bed."

"Yes, but it wasn't a *marriage* bed before today. We just magically turned it into one, or at least we will when we officially consummate our marriage in it."

"Well, yes, I suppose so." She studied Amy's face. "It's been a good party though, hasn't it?"

"It has, although I'm pretty sure your mom's high-brow literary friends are all wondering how you got stuck with me."

"How *did* I get stuck with you?" Lira teased.

Amy gave her a look of mock offense. "Well you *are* stuck with me now. This ring says so." She took Lira's hand. "Shall we go?"

"Yes, I think so. But we should say goodbye first, shouldn't we?"

"Nah. I think everyone will figure out where we went." She squeezed Lira's hand. "I say we just run."

Lira lit up. "Like we're escaping criminals or something?"

Amy laughed. "So we're starting the role play right now, are we?" She kissed Lira's cheek. "Yes. Exactly like escaping criminals."

"We could be prison cell mates who formed a relationship and are now escaping together," Lira suggested excitedly.

"Yes. In our wedding dresses, which we had on in jail."

Lira made a face at her.

"We'll work it out in the car," Amy promised. "Now let's *run*."

So they ran.

ABOUT THE AUTHOR

Michelle Arnold grew up in Illinois, two blocks from her local library, where she spent a lot of time as a child. She began writing stories around the age of six and never stopped, although the quality has greatly improved since then. She graduated from the University of Illinois in 2004 and has since worked in the field of education while continuing to write. So far she has published two novels, *After Raya* and *The World The Way It Should Be*, and a short story, "Haunting Lia." This is her first crime novel, but given her lasting obsession with shows like *Criminal Minds*, it was only a matter of time.

Ms. Arnold currently resides in Illinois with her cat, Lily Belle.

47074145R00119

Made in the USA
San Bernardino, CA
11 August 2019